Sand Storm

Wildcat Wizard Book 11

Get deals and new releases notifications first via the
newsletter www.alkline.co.uk

Memories

The bloodshot eyes of Zewedu spilled spectral tears onto my kitchen tiles. The gaping maw of my dead teacher stretched so wide that his cracked lips split. His crooked teeth, what few remained, tumbled from his mouth silently, like urine-soaked icicles falling from a particularly grubby roof. His fat tongue poked around the cavernous interior as if searching for the yellow canines before the disembodied head let rip with a blood-curdling scream that forced me to cover my ears.

Penelope dropped a pan of just-boiled potatoes she was about to drain into the sink. Hands on hips, she turned and shouted above the din, "Can you get it to stop? This is utterly annoying."

"Wish I could," I hollered, meaning it with all my heart.

Zewedu's ghost, or ghost-memory, spirit, or merely the lingering magical emanations of a once-powerful wizard, whatever it was, screamed again as more ethereal tears fell before he snapped out of existence and the kitchen was ours once more.

"Ugh, this is doing my head in," I moaned as I grabbed the back of a chair then lowered myself slowly. I rested my elbows on the table and cupped my chin in my hands, mostly just to check my head was still attached and not about to float about the room like Zewedu's.

"What about me?" screeched my darling wife. "You know all about this stuff, I don't. He keeps coming into the bathroom! He popped out of the bin earlier. I caught that damn head hiding behind the shower curtain yesterday. Scared the life out of me. Can't you do something?" Penelope recovered the pan after scowling at me like it was all my fault. Luckily, the potatoes were still inside, but she had to clean up the mess. She made sure I knew it too, what with all the tutting.

When she was finished, she came and sat opposite me. I didn't even have the heart to tell her she'd missed a spot. That's how unnerved I was by the whole thing.

"Arthur, this has been going on for over a week now. I'm all for you doing your tricks and getting into mischief—"

"They aren't tricks," I protested.

"But," continued Penelope, "this is too much. I can't have floating heads in the house, it's not right. You need to do something, and today. No more heads," she warned.

She had a point. It wasn't exactly normal, and it wasn't even abnormal but fun, it was just annoying, a bit depressing, and somewhat worrying, not that I'd told my wife that. George had become fed up with it too, meaning I was getting an ear-bashing from both wonderful ladies almost constantly, and that did nothing to ease my nerves, quite the opposite.

I knew I had to do the thing I was about to tell Penelope, but I'd been trying to avoid it, to think of another way. Now I knew there was only one course of action left, and boy would it suck.

"I have to go on a trip," I said with a sigh.

"What trip? We've only just returned from honeymoon. Weeks, that's all."

"I know, and I don't want to go, but it's the only way."

"Arthur Salzman, stop talking in riddles."

"Sorry. Zewedu is calling to me, I have to go. Something's wrong."

"You said it was just a ghost-memory thing, that it would go away soon."

"I know, and I hoped it would. But he won't. So I have to go on a trip."

"Where? How long for?"

I looked my wife, my beautiful, perfect, extremely understanding wife in the eyes and said, "I'm going to the desert, to Ethiopia, and as for how long I'll be gone, I have no idea."

Hi, I'm Arthur "The Hat" Salzman. Gangster. Wizard. About to get sand in all my crevices.

Stupid Planes

Airplanes suck.

Bit Hot

After I'd been squeezed into spaces only suitable for tiny children, and forced to sit next to several overfed men who refused to let me use the arm rest even once, and had to breathe recycled air for hours upon end, it was with great relief, and much creaking, that I disembarked from the flying torture device and rushed through the airport, longing for the bustling streets of Dire Dawa. Anything was preferable to the toxic airport, the same the world over. Stinking of perfume, chocolate, and bleach, everything gleaming and fake, so far from a true representation of how the hundred and ten million Ethiopians lived it wasn't even funny.

It had taken me three flights, two days, and more meals heated by gamma rays than can be good for you to get here, and I felt bloody awful.

My lips were dry, my face felt more wrinkled than usual, like there were actual creases in it, and some of it was peeling off in long strips. I was like a dried banana.

But I'd made it, and there had only been a single incident when Zewedu made an appearance on the last flight, much to the surprise then amusement of the other passengers who seemed to think that somehow very realistic 3D holograms had finally been invented and a budget airline was the first to get to try them out.

Whatever, it was done. I just had to figure out a way to get several thousand miles home without leaving the ground, which was tricky but I was positive there had to be a better way. Certainly one that didn't involve all circulation to your legs being cut off and risking thrombosis.

I removed Grace and wiped at my head with a bandanna. Flakes of skin stuck to it, which was gross.

"Fucking Zewedu," I moaned, the heat tearing at my cracked lips. My raspy throat had what little moisture remained sucked from it as African heat wormed its way inside me and I craved a dry sauna for some relief. Damn, how did people live in places like this? Give me rainy England any day. I think this was more me stressing out than the true heat I remembered in the desert. Dire Dawa wasn't even that hot, but after England it felt like an inferno.

But I had been here before, many years ago, and had stayed for well over a year, learning much of what I now knew, or at least being taught the means by which I could improve my skills over the many intervening years. More years than I cared to think about. Where had the time gone? So much time, so many fights, so many artifacts, so much magic. So many lonely nights, tossing and turning, the mini death never coming, lying in the dark wondering what the fuck I was doing with my life.

Then George came and things were better than I could have ever hoped, and then I bumped into Penelope and I realized in an instant that she was what I'd been searching for my whole life. It wasn't the magic that made me whole, made me truly feel alive, it was her. She was the missing part of me, she made everything better, even made living bearable.

Life was perfect now. Sure, there were missing friends and bad guys out to hurt little girls, Cerberus was waging an ongoing war with Ivan and the vampires and anyone else not a regular citizen, and the new leader had surprised us all, breaking Ivan's heart along the way. The magical underworld was in uproar because of it, but that was all par for the course. I was happy, content, and now Zewedu, a dead Ethiopian who had been a pain in the ass when alive, even more so decades after I killed him, was ruining it all.

Not that it was actually him, of course, he was dead and I presumed buried, I hadn't hung around to find out, but if this headless version of his life force, which was mighty potent, was being so insistent, then I had to interrupt my perfect life to come see what all the fuss was about.

Memories flooded back, things I hadn't thought about for many years, things that once upon a time had kept me awake at night, not with guilt, but with regret that maybe the old bugger could have taught me more, had secrets still to share. But I'd ended his life as I knew he wanted. There had been an unspoken agreement between us that he had taught me all I could learn and we were no longer master and student, some would say master and servant, but I was if not his equal then certainly after a year of teaching and study well on my way to becoming an adept.

Zewedu wasn't big on talking, never praised me or told me how I was progressing, something I'd been accustomed to after living with those two people who called themselves my parents but acted like I was a stranger. He was big on hitting, with a very hard stick. We did lots of sitting and staring on the thankfully cool, compacted earth in his tiny but neat and very sparse home carved from the ancient desert rock.

Desert, all that existed was desert, and us, alone in a cave, me getting the shit kicked out of me day after day, but it had all been worth it for I had sought this out for so long. Roamed the earth in search of answers to questions I didn't even know I had, and he had helped me find the answers and given me more than I could have ever imagined.

They were not happy times but they were the happiest of times, for I was learning magic and I would have put up with anything, and did, to master such wonders. I suffered, I grew painfully thin, almost as thin as my master. We often starved, we were always sore, or I was, covered in bruises, and the work we did was dangerous beyond belief, for magic is not for the faint of heart. It can tear you apart, consume your mind and leave you utterly mad, which I truly think was the case with Zewedu. But he reveled in his madness, and I loved every hate-filled minute of it.

A tug at my sleeve, and why the hell was I still wearing my leather jacket? interrupted my reverie.

"You want taxi, mister? I got best in city," said a boy of maybe twelve wearing grubby shorts, green flip flops, and a dirty vest. He looked at me with beautiful dark eyes, hope-filled, and smiled, baring gleaming teeth.

"You aren't old enough to drive," I said, shaking him loose and removing my jacket.

"Tee-hee, I'm not the driver, he is." The boy pointed to a man in a sorry looking excuse for a car, an ancient sedan covered in dirt and dust. Someone had scribbled doodles into the crud with their finger, making it look even dirtier.

"And what, you kidnap me and steal my stuff? No thanks."

"No kidnapping, just a ride to nice hotel. You want nice hotel? I know plenty. Clean sheets, hot water, even get lady to do the nooky nooky if you want." The child wiggled his eyebrows suggestively.

Why is it in every country I go to there is an utterly cliched person of some description there to greet me? Maybe that's why they're cliched, because it really is like this. Kids out to earn extra cash, help out the families, I couldn't hold that against him. He was trying to earn enough so his family could eat. What a different world this was to back home, and I reminded myself not to forget it. This country was huge, had suffered so much it was impossible to comprehend, and life was very different here. A struggle, the whole nation had been struggling for so long they knew no other way.

"Hey, mister, you do that a lot? You zone out much?"

"Yeah, now and then," I said with a smile. "Okay, grab this," I handed him my bag, "and don't steal anything."

"I'm a professional," he said, affronted, then heaved my pack over his shoulder and keenly led me to the "taxi."

Welcome Home

I gave the boy a nice tip which he was delighted with, then told the taxi driver where I wanted to go. He took off like a rocket without thrust control and soon we were hurtling through downtown Dire Dawa, that is, until we hit downtown proper, then we mostly crawled slower than I could have walked. He weaved between the throngs, swiped other vehicles, dodged thousands of people riding scooters and motorbikes, most having never heard of safety gear or that flip-flops weren't the best choice of footwear, and carrying long lengths of timber wasn't ideal on a two-wheeled motorized vehicle, and generally added to the pollution as he honked his horn incessantly and hummed happily to himself as the meter continued to roll over.

By the time we arrived at the small hotel I was ready for someone to shoot me in the head, because the driver had begun to sing along, badly, to Euro-pop from a cassette he was pleased to tell me he'd made himself by recording from the radio.

I paid him, tipped him, and grabbed my things as he tore away through a gap in the traffic—at least by Ethiopian standards it was a gap.

I stood on the street and admired the facade of the building. It looked the same. Maybe a few more patches of render were missing, maybe the green windows were a little worse for wear, but the sign still hung same as it always had, and the smells were the same too. Could she still be here after all these years? Only one way to find out.

A Familiar Face

I pushed open the ornately carved door, older than me, and walked along a narrow, cool passageway, everything so familiar the intervening years slipped away. I smiled as I emerged into a large courtyard where every surface was covered in tiny blue tiles, the fountain gurgled away happily, and tropical plants reached for the sky. It was shaded by the balconies above that ran around the perimeter, with places to sit and soak up the muted noise of the city and enjoy the rare damp air.

So peaceful, so beautiful, so perfect.

I took a seat and let the frustration of the trip fade away, replaced with fond memories of this place. When it was over with Zewedu, I'd roamed for months in the desert, a nomad with no place to call home, no true friends, no place in this world. A true outcast. I'd isolated myself from what was normal, followed a path to madness, and that madness had taken a firm grip on me once I'd learned my craft. I battled the desert and just about won after wandering the scorched earth until

I was black from the sun and a husk of a man, nothing left inside but a thousand spells whirling around my system, crying for release.

Oh, and what release there was.

Alone in the freezing desert at night, billions of stars watching, I let loose with unbelievable light shows of magnificent fury. I tore up the sky and gazed in wonder at my own hands, shocked by their ability, their potential for damage. I reveled in it, loved it, and the desert purged me until finally I was clean.

Then I came back to the city and I found the Oasis, and what an oasis it was.

"I smell white man," came a booming voice that woke me from a slumber I didn't know had taken me.

I shook away the sleep and readied for action.

A smile spread as I stood to watch a vision of loveliness stride with purpose towards me across the courtyard, proud head held high, nose twitching. Sameena's eyes glinted with mirth and mischief, the colorful scarf covering her hair shook as her head wobbled slightly side to side like it used to in the old days. Her face was darker than my cold heart, the skin had ignored time, unmarred and flawless apart from ancient tribal scars given to her when but a child, not a wrinkle to be seen. They say fat people age better, and it was true. She was a large woman by anyone's standards but her own, and I could see that she hadn't lost her appetite, had gained more if anything, and it showed.

Sameena looked great, awesome in fact. Her huge, swishing, brightly-colored gown like a tent on acid flapped about as if caught by a breeze, rippled as her folds of flesh wobbled beneath. She was the picture of health, a rare sight indeed in a country where so many never knew where their next meal was coming from.

"You don't look a day over forty," I said as I held out my hands.

"And you look like you have had many adventures," she replied politely, her accent thicker than I recalled.

"Haha, you could say that."

My old friend, now well into her sixties, ignored my outstretched hands and hugged me tight. It felt good, soft and warm, and she smelled of spices, just as I remembered.

"It is excellent to see you, Arthur. I have heard tales of your exploits even from this remote corner of the earth."

"Nothing good, I hope." We released from our embrace and stood back to inspect each other. It took me longer than her, I had a lot more to inspect.

"All very interesting." Sameena frowned. "And why has it taken you so long to come visit me?"

"You know how it is. I hadn't planned on ever coming back, but I had no choice."

"Ah, the head?" she asked, nodding over my shoulder.

"Yeah, the head," I sighed. I turned to see Zewedu's face giving me the evil eye.

"Get out of here, damn spirit," shrieked Sameena, scaring everything within a hundred-mile radius. Even the fountain paused then resumed its splashing once it recovered from the shock.

Zewedu's mouth opened in a silent scream before he vanished. Sameena was one formidable woman.

"So, what's new?" I asked, grinning like a fool.

"Much has changed, but much remains the same. War, poverty, corruption at every turn. It is the way of things here."

"Sounds just like I remember. And business? Place is looking great, just as it was."

"Business is the usual mix of quiet times and busy times. I make do best I can. Try to count my blessings, be grateful for what I have worked hard to achieve. I am a lucky woman."

"You were always a hard worker. You looked after me back then, helped me so much. I can never tell you how grateful I am."

"Haha, you silly boy. I was happy to help. You were a starving, wild-eyed wreck when you stumbled into this courtyard, but I could see it, that light in your eyes, in your heart. Your spirit shone bright and I knew I had to save this boy who arrived full of magic and madness."

"And you did. You fed me, cared for me, showed me how things could be."

"And you have done well."

"Maybe. I've done a few things right but I've got plenty wrong too. I've done bad things, Sameena, so much death and hurt."

"Ah, but such is the life of one like you. Wizards walk a fine line between good and evil. They take a different path to the rest. It is a madness that consumes you all, this need to be apart from other people, to master the wildness. It takes a certain kind of person to want that, let alone to not be eaten away by such foolishness. So, yes, you have done well."

"Thanks. Ah, it's so good to see you. I can't believe it's been so many years."

"What are the years but the passing of seasons? They mean nothing, just the chance for new beginnings, for new life to enter the world and for the old to make way for the growing young. It is the way of things, nothing more, nothing less."

"You always were a wise woman. Now," I said, hardly able to contain myself, "I hope your cooking is as good as it was. I'm starving."

"My cooking," Sameena spread her arms wide and smiled her beautiful smile, "has improved, as you can see."

"What, you look as perfect as always. Wouldn't change a thing about you."

"Too kind, too kind. Come, I will show you to your room. Relax a while, and Sameena will cook you something that will make you wonder why you ever left."

I nodded. Sometimes I wondered why I did leave, but this was not my home, I didn't belong. And yet, right now I felt like I was exactly where I should be, which was worrying.

A Moment

The room was compact but nicely furnished, a mix of traditional Ethiopian style with a few modern twists. Nothing expensive, just presented well with little touches by Sameena that gave it a homely feel. The bed was firm bordering on being a rock, but the fresh sheets were cool and as I lay there, hands laced behind my head, I felt peace.

My thoughts drifted back to when I first came here, which was why I didn't want to come, at least in part. I didn't want to dredge up the past, to think about how life was back then. How I was, the things I did, the life that came before. Even after Sameena sorted me out, I was still a crazed child in many regards, not fully becoming a man for many years.

But she saved me from myself, planted the seeds of change, gave me a chance at a future. Without her I would have been dead within a year or two, I knew that for sure, as I was utterly obsessed with magic, had been living in a damn cave with an insane man for a year then almost beaten by the desert. She fed me, cared for me, tended my wounds, and cured, or almost cured, my crazed mind.

Still wild, just not mental.

I guess I saw Sameena as the mother I never had but desperately wanted. I may have only been with her for a matter of weeks but she did more for me in that time than any other woman had in my life up to that point. Sure, when I left I made plenty of mistakes, like hooking up with George's mum for one, but even that had a silver lining, so who knows, life has a funny way of surprising you no matter how hard you try to steer it in a certain direction.

I heard the talk about Sameena back then, that she was a dangerous woman. Several called her bad, and others, those brave or foolish enough to think she would never find out, even commented on her weight, saying it wasn't right she was so big when others were starving. She had come up the hard way, struggled for everything she had, worked damn hard and she loved her food. So given the opportunity, having known true hunger in her youth, having starved like much of the country, she ate, a lot.

Should she give all her money away, feed others? Some would say yes, she should, but those talking about her were the ones doing so over a beer in some bar or other. They drove cars, lived in the city, and were far removed from what was going on in the vast rural areas of the country. Sameena helped many people, did plenty of good work, she just didn't brag about it. She did her bit and more besides, so who were they to judge? I certainly didn't, not when I came from another country where the amount of food wasted was criminal and we were in no position to pass comment, our lives unbelievably privileged compared to the majority of those in this beautiful, dynamic, terrifying, incredibly poor, ravaged country.

Some problems were too big for the likes of me, and I knew myself well enough to know that I would never do anything about such epic crimes. Crimes committed by so many of us on a truly global scale, so I certainly didn't get to decide how others lived.

I let the memories sail by without paying them much heed as that way lay a true kind of madness, and just drifted on a haze of warmth and familiarity. The noise of the city drifted in through the windows, but I focused on the fountain and the cool courtyard and soon enough I sank deep into a fitful slumber deserving of kings.

When I awoke, it was to find the night had crept into the room and wrapped me in it's uncaring embrace. I smiled, feeling refreshed and ravenous. So before I headed into the unknown, revisited old haunts where ghosts of the past waited for me, I padded barefoot down into the courtyard to visit the only friendly ghost this country would offer me.

Sound and smell hit long before I laid eyes on the feast that awaited. Others were already tucking in to the spread laid out on several tables, with Sameena helping serve, laughing and joking with her guests. This was how she always did it. A communal meal once a day for anyone who wanted to partake, for other meals you had to fend for yourself.

I greeted Sameena warmly, her smile infectious as always, then I sat with strangers and ate food not of this world, chatting, laughing, and enjoying the good company. The group included people from not only Africa but from Germany, Spain, a lovely couple from Brazil, and others whose faces and nationality I forget but whose spirit I will always remember for their kindness and for the lovely evening they allowed me to share.

And then it was over, like a dream that ended too suddenly, and I was dragged from my comfortable numbness as I found myself alone in the courtyard. The weight of Africa descended on me as every bad thing that had happened here came flooding back.

That's life for you. It's great for a while then it returns to being shit for much longer. It's why you have to hold on to the good times, as there's usually a bloody long break before the next one.

Grumpy? Me? Maybe, but I know too much about the black hearts of humanity to ever be jolly for too long.

Vicky sprang into my mind as I sat looking up at the stars. She'd hate that I came without her, but this was no place for her. This was no place for me.

On the Road Again

Wizards travel light. I had a small rucksack—suitcases on wheels are no good for those of us who need to run away fast—the clothes on my back, and pockets full of random items I might or might not need. Main thing was they were there if I did need them, although what exactly was secreted away in the dark depths of my combats and jacket was up for debate.

What I didn't have was company. After a teary farewell, I waved to Sameena as I left in the same dirty taxi I arrived in. Throughout the day and night I traveled by tiny, terrifying airplane, motorbike, bus, a donkey for a little while, but that's another story, and then finally, with no other option, I stopped at the last town, one so rundown it didn't even have a name, before everything turned to desert and hired a beat-up 4×4 that could cope with the sand and the heat even if it had no air con.

Now I was truly alone. No Vicky, no Penelope or George, no Steve, not even my faery godmother. She'd been quiet of late, had hardly made an appearance, and

I wondered if she was mad with me. Doubtful, probably just off doing fae stuff as was often the case. Sometimes it was months before I saw her, then it was like she'd never been gone. Actually, it was probably because I was being cautious, not risking my life in such a gung-ho manner, so she hadn't had to bail me out for a while. Not since I found out about the contract, so maybe that was it.

I tried to relax as I bumped my way slowly along what the locals optimistically referred to as a road. I called it many things but certainly nothing as polite as that. I was clenching my teeth, my neck hurt, and the damn heat was intolerable. Worse than that though was that every time I gripped the steering wheel with both hands a fly would time it to perfection to land on my nose and annoy the hell out of me. Then every time I swatted one away it would coincide perfectly with a pothole so I'd jar my spine and the whole process would be repeated over, and over, and over again.

I drove on through the afternoon, into the evening and the darkness of the vast, endless desert as night descended.

You don't know true darkness until you've stood under an African sky and stared up into infinity. It's humbling, beautiful beyond compare, and utterly terrifying. If you think you're alone now just try it and you'll soon realize how small and inconsequential you really are.

So I skipped that and kept the lights on, even played some music, because no way did I want to feel less worthy of life than I did at this moment.

On I drove, heading towards my past, nothing but a disgruntled head for sporadic company, increasing his visits the closer we got.

My jaw ached, my hands gripped the steering wheel, my thoughts became as dark as the desert and just as cold.

This region of Africa was a mass of contradictions. The heat intolerable during the day, making me crave the cooler city, the nights frigid and raw. Hospitable yet unfriendly, the people hungry yet always smiling, the governments corrupt yet many of the leaders loved by the people. And here I was, a stranger, an intruder, come to make everything worse.

I opened the window and tasted the ancient desert, breathed in the dry air that bore motes of our ancestors, tiny bits of humanity ground to dust, then I screamed into the night. A hyena replied to my cry for help. Maybe he was alone too; maybe he liked it that way.

Bloody Typical

I had no map, there was certainly no sat nav, and I had no phone as I'd purposely left it behind, not that there would be a signal here anyway. I needed none of it, knew exactly where I was headed and how to get there. I was like a bird that could fly halfway around the world and land in the same tree every year, traveling by the magnetic pull of the earth itself, by the stars, by instinct.

There was no need to think about it, I took in the information on a subconscious level and was merely guided towards the old village.

By now the road was long gone, not even faint tire tracks to show me the way. The desert scoured the land clean every night when the winds howled across the plains and the dunes crept across the barren land, ever moving, nothing stationary here although it looked like it hadn't changed in a million years.

On I drove, nothing but me and the wild animals, startled by the lights of the vehicle, skipping away down tracks used by their ancestors, the routes mapped out for them as clearly as if they were lit by street lights.

The vehicle juddered. I panicked, checking the fuel gauge but it was still half full since I'd not long topped it up from the jerry cans stacked in the back, so it wasn't that. I eased up but it got worse, the accelerator only worked intermittently and then it refused to respond at all. The car slowed and then with a final cough the engine died. The lights cut out and I was plunged into darkness.

Immediately, a chill entered the truck as the night wrapped around tight, so I sat there, smiling, knowing Africa would do its best to claim me for good this time.

"Bring it on, old friend. I'm ready."

It Begins

Rule number one. Never challenge the desert. I should have known better, because it responded to my cockiness.

As I exited the truck to maybe check the engine, or kick the tires or something, the wind picked up and fierce, freezing gusts pelted me like icicles. I staggered against the onslaught as the door slammed shut, leaving me yanking at the handle but unable to beat the weather.

I turned to confront the night and Grace was blown from my head like she wasn't held in place with wards that had worked under more extreme conditions than this to keep her secured. I snatched her from the air before she was lost for good and doggedly rammed her back into place, beefing up the wards as I did so. No way would I go out without my hat on my head, it wouldn't be seemly.

The wind tore at my jacket, it eddied and flowed, rose then fell, swept underneath my arms and tried to lift me from the ground. I grunted as I bent forward and headed towards the village still several miles to the east. Sand scraped my exposed skin, wearing away the hairs on the back of my hands until I stuffed them into my pockets. I kept my head down, walked by instinct alone, and let the night do its worst.

Cold beyond belief, finding it hard to breathe, and really wishing there was a cafe nearby for a nice fry up and a coffee, I doggedly strode into the night.

I felt alive. I'd truly returned now.

New Beginnings

The storm passed eventually and left silence in its wake. A deep, endless silence, not a car horn, a shout, a siren to be heard. Not even the soft coo of a pigeon.

As the sun rose over the horizon, warmth flooded my veins. The sand shimmered as though made of molten glass.

I looked skyward as a screech broke the peace. Vultures hovered overhead, peering down at the intruder to see how soon it would succumb and they could feast.

"Not today, I'm afraid. The Hat has unfinished business here."

I marched towards the rising sun and my fate.

Where it all Began

It was a little past eight in the morning when I arrived at the outskirts of the village. There wasn't much left of it now. Small hillocks on the otherwise flat, dusty ground signaled where the thatched huts once stood, most abandoned even before I'd first arrived apart from a few stalwarts who clung to the old ways and remained until they passed. Now the old homes were nothing but brittle piles of twigs poking from desiccated earth.

Fire pits were still in evidence, circles of rocks with hollow centers like lunar craters covered in a dusting of sand.

I wandered around slowly, not expecting to find anything but searching nonetheless. A graveyard of abandoned history, this way of life still common for millions upon millions but there was no future for them living like this and if they could leave they did. It didn't always end up better, crammed into cities, living in poverty, no jobs, no money, no hope, but many tried and they would keep on trying. Looking for something more, believing there was something more. Just the promise of running water was enough to lure people away from places like this. Who would choose to walk for half a day to collect water when you could turn on a tap in the room you lived in?

It was eerie. Not even wild dogs picked through the remains. Everything had been wiped clean.

I took in the looming, craggy rock face off in the distance where people had made cool, insulated homes for themselves for millennia until superstition made them abandon them, and where I had lived with Zewedu. I hadn't looked until now as I knew once I did then I would see nothing else, drawn to it like a moth to a flame.

With a sigh, and a wipe of my forehead, I set off once more, wondering what I would find, why I was here.

I wished I'd packed sandwiches.

Could be Worse

I made the climb up steps carved into rock that I'd done thousands of times before. I forgot how crap it was. By the time I reached the door, I was sweating worse than a hippo in a volcano. I stood panting and soaked as I fumbled for the water bottle. After draining half, I stashed it in a pocket then checked the crumbling door for wards.

Zewedu's wards still worked perfectly so there was little chance anyone had been inside since his death. Damn, this would be grisly. I'd killed him right inside the doorway in the sparse living room. The wards had been modified to allow me entry and the access remained, so I turned the doorknob and flinched despite my resolve.

With a suitably eerie creak, all part of Zewedu's magic and there for effect only, the door eased open and the gloomy interior was revealed, sickly light entering through the small windows either side of the door.

Now, you'd think maybe the smell would hit, that it would stink to high heaven after Zewedu's corpse being entombed for so long and the room being closed off, but the windows were just holes, no glass needed, and the temperature was always pretty constant here in the mountain. Sure, it was rather musty, and could do with a little air freshener, a quick spray with something toxic that in no way smelled of pine trees, but it could have been worse.

The room was lit by a half-light that never changed during the day, shadowed by the overhang outside, but I saw well enough.

There on the floor, dead as dead could be, was the desiccated corpse of Zewedu. There was no moisture here, everything was dry as a bone, and slowly, over the years, all liquid in his body had been sucked out of him. Zewedu had been skinny in life and he looked almost the same size now. His skin was like leather, dark with a dull shine as though he'd been polished in places. Sand had banked up against one side as it blew through the windows as though his burial had begun then been abandoned.

Naked, which was how he usually was, I could see that animals had taken a few nibbles, but it was mostly ants that had stolen his flesh, probably helped preserve the body by sucking the juices out of him soon after death. His wards had stopped anything larger doing much damage and even now I sensed the faint traces of protection lingering around his corpse like a dog refusing to leave its master.

It was the head that got to me. The wound in his neck was a mere hole where I'd ended his life, puckered and dark as his open mouth. His dreadlocks trailed away across the compacted earth, great coils of rope almost silver. His eyes were shut but his mouth gaped wide just like in his disembodied appearances and I kept expecting something gross to pop out but it never happened.

I skirted the body carefully, loathe to disturb him from his permanent slumber, and inspected the rest of the house. There wasn't much to see. The rudimentary kitchen area, little more than a fire pit and a few pots and pans, bowls for washing up in. The rest of the room was empty save for several rugs and a wooden chair he refused to let us ever use.

The bathroom and bedroom were just as devoid of anything interesting, so I returned to the main space and stood inspecting the old man, wondering why I was here, kind of glad I couldn't ask him but knowing I had to get an answer from somewhere or what was the point of all this?

With little else to do, I sat cross-legged on the ground and leaned back against the cool rock wall. For maybe an hour, maybe longer, I did nothing but wait, watching my old master as I contemplated the possible reasons for his call. There was nothing that came to mind that made any sense, nothing I could dredge up from my memory that warranted this insistent beckoning. I knew when I killed him that it was what he wanted, that he was finally afraid and couldn't do it himself. I'd done it without a moment's hesitation, so deeply entrenched was I in the world he'd created, the two of us alone for so long. Close, so close to each other yet the distance had been huge, his strange nature making it impossible for us to connect and show any signs of affection.

I was brimming with magic then, untamed and dangerous, and utterly under his thrall. Yet I'd still known it was time to leave so that's what I did. Now I'd returned and it was doing me no favors, merely making me depressed when I thought of the man I had been, the things I endured under his ever-watchful rheumy eyes.

"What do you want, you old goat?" I whispered, disturbing dust motes that spun lazily then sailed away towards the windows.

The head shot through, in no way disturbing the passing dust, and then the door slammed shut. Darkness became total then was replaced with a silver glow that spread out from the corpse like the ground was freezing. And it was bloody cold, the temperature plummeted and I shivered, so welcome after the heat.

The head twisted as it glided to the center of the room then it spun around and around impossibly fast before the mouth opened wider than ever before and Zewedu's scream pierced the very fabric of my being and set my teeth rattling.

Faster and faster, nothing but a blur, and then it suddenly stopped, stared me right in the eye, then gently, as if to ensure I was watching and understood, it dipped forward and pointed at the ground before it sank right through. Spectral dreadlocks slithered through the earth until they too were gone and nothing remained but one old man and one very dead wizard.

"Subtle, dude, very subtle."

With a sigh, I clambered to my feet, looked down at Zewedu, and said, "I'll go get that spade then, shall I?" Thankfully, he didn't answer.

Bit Ominous

As I dug deeper with the fold-up shovel I'd paid a fortune for into the surprisingly soft ground, I got the uncomfortable impression I was digging my own grave. I'd expected hard rock just beneath the grainy surface I'd been made to sweep daily but the loose dirt mixed with the ashes of countless fires just went deeper and deeper. I dug out bits of charcoal, pieces of bone from meals long ago consumed, and more than a few things I peered at suspiciously then discarded as of no import.

There was a lot of hair, from long fine threads to whole lengths of dreadlock, and I even found a sandal. But I hadn't been shown where to dig just to reclaim crap footwear, there was a real purpose to this and so I continued.

I flung earth away into the corners of the room, coughing and spluttering, necking water, and generally muttering under my breath the whole time.

The hole grew large and long, and when I clambered out for a breather I realized I really had dug a grave, a bloody deep one at that. Was this why I was here, to give the old man a decent burial after all these years? Surely not. He was happy where he was, wasn't he?

"Are you? Are you okay there or do you want to go in?" I asked.

The door rattled in its frame.

"I'll take that as a no, shall I? Or was it a yes?"

The door rattled twice.

"Fine, be like that. Hell, look what you've done. I've only been here a few hours and already I'm going a bit mad, talking like you're still alive. Well, you aren't, you're dead, and I thought that would make you happy."

The door rattled three times; there was no pleasing some people.

I eyed the hole with suspicion then with a wipe of my brow I hopped back inside and continued to dig. Maybe I'd reach hell eventually, maybe I was already there.

I hardly rested throughout the day, I dug through the afternoon and evening, and then I stopped because I couldn't see anything.

Rather than return to the truck for the portable lights, I released the Velcro at my pocket and pulled out Wand.

"About time! What's your game leaving me in there when there's adventure to be had?" he moaned.

"Been busy, didn't want any distractions. And besides, this is personal."

"Personal, I'm you, you're me, we are the—"

"We're the same, blah, blah, blah," I interrupted, having heard the lecture many times before.

"No need for that," he said with a sulk and a droop of his head. Yeah, I know, he's a stick, tell him that.

"Look, are you going to give me some light so I can work, or not?"

"Fine, but don't put me away again, not unless I'm sleepy," he added.

"Whatever."

I released Wand and he lit up like it was bloody Christmas as he hovered above my head. White lights flashed on and off, inducing an instant headache. "Seriously?"

"Spoilsport."

Wand switched to a more muted glow, still with a series of small lights running along his length, but it would have to do. I continued to dig, wondering just how deep this mystery went.

Clonk.

The spade hit something hard but hollow-sounding. I bent and peered at the item as I wiped away the dirt. It was a small box, nothing special, but I was sure the contents would be.

I dug around the edges then pulled on tiny handles either side and lifted it out of the ground. It weighed next to nothing, made no sound, and I wondered if this was just Zewedu's idea of a joke. He'd always had a dark sense of humor, reveled in my discomfort, and had me doing countless things I later discovered were for no other reason than his own amusement at my suffering.

"A little more light?" I asked Wand. He came closer as if to take a look and we both peered at the nondescript lid of a simple wooden box, gray with age and brittle as Zewedu's desiccated toenails, which were disgustingly long now.

I used the spade to prize the lid off, jumping back as it came free for fear of a long-forgotten spell being unleashed and chewing out my brain or something really nasty.

Nothing happened.

"Scaredy-cat," I scolded Wand as he slowly approached after darting away into a corner.

"Can never be too careful," he said sheepishly.

We peered into the box. There was a piece of paper. Yellow and curled up at the edges.

I lifted it out carefully. It was a detailed drawing of the surrounding area, complete with dunes, rocky outcroppings, and the craggy mountains.

There was an X marked right in the middle of nowhere, in the huge desert several miles from here where the ground never saw rain and nobody went because there was nothing to see.

"Seriously, Zewedu? A fucking treasure hunt?"

Guess I knew what I was doing next.

Not the Best Sleep

There was no point tearing off into the desert in the middle of the night. For one, I had no truck, two, I was hungry and had to find food, three, it would be scary.

By the light of Wand, I gingerly descended from the hellhole of pirate treasure maps and did my damnedest not to trip on the steps and go arse over tit into oblivion. That would be typical, dying here with nobody finding me for decades, looking just like Zewedu but with a nice hat. His hat, in fact.

Safely down on terra firma, I headed off a little ways into the desert and then sat my bony bum down on the sand.

"What we waiting for?" asked Wand.

"I thought you were me, I was you?"

"Just making conversation. Shall I dim the lights?"

I stared at my idiot companion. Damn, it was like having Vicky with me. Ah, that was it, he was making up for it, doing things he knew I secretly enjoyed. Like making fun of Vicky's height, or lack of it, and her penchant for kids' jumpers.

"Thanks," I said gruffly.

"Welcome." Wand dimmed his lights and we waited.

It didn't take long. About fifteen minutes later a small rabbit came to investigate the light. As soon as it was close enough I gripped Wand, felt my will surge into him, then shot out a slender blast of darkest death like a javelin that killed the creature without suffering.

I took my prize back to the village and scavenged wood from the old hut roofs before bundling it up and carrying it up the steps.

Once inside, and wondering why I hadn't stayed out in the open where there were no ghosts, and no dried-up bodies either, I nonetheless set about making a fire. Once it was burning nicely, I skinned the rabbit with my trusty pocket knife, chopped it up, and used some of its own fat to smear an old cast iron pan before setting it to cook.

Sinking to my haunches, I stared into the flames of the small fire that sent orange light dancing across the uneven walls. A familiar smell of smoke and grease filled my nostrils and I smiled. Maybe I should have never left. Maybe I should have stayed here, lived simply, remained apart from the complications of modern life like Zewedu had.

No, this wasn't my place, I belonged somewhere now, my search was finally over, and I would return home no matter what.

The flames flickered, the smoke was sucked out through the cleverly designed hole in the rock far above, and I watched the fire, lost to times long gone.

I burned the rabbit, but it still tasted delicious. I ate like a caveman, using my fingers. Grease dripped down my wrists, soaked into my beard, and ran down my chin. It was the best damn meal I'd had in years.

Plus, and total bonus, no need to bother washing up. I threw the remains of the meal, pan and all, into the pit and covered them over. With dust and grease having turned me into the ash man, I returned to the fire and sat there, full of belly, dirty and stinking of smoke.

"Just like old times, eh?" I asked, turning to Zewedu.

An eye opened, stared right at me, as rheumy and bloodshot as ever.

"Haha, good one. Guess you still have a few tricks left to play on your old student, eh?"

The eyelid closed and I returned to stare at the flames.

The dead can't hurt you. Usually.

At some point tiredness overcame me, jet lag with a vengeance. I downed the rest of the water then relaxed on the ground, curled up tight to keep warm as the fire slowly died.

My sleep was fitful, filled with nightmares of being buried alive, of being trapped in the room until I starved, gnawing on Zewedu's leathery corpse for sustenance but finding it was devoid of anything but maggots lurking under the hide. Their skins popped as I chewed them and warm liquid oozed down my throat.

I awoke with a start, panicked that I was trapped, but I was just caught up in my jacket sleeves. Once I extricated myself, I pushed the last of the wood into the embers and blew hard until the fire was resurrected. Rubbing my hands together, I got the circulation going before standing and taking in the room.

"Fine, I'll do it, but you better say thank you."

I arched my back until it cracked then picked up the shovel, flattened out the base of the trench, then dragged Zewedu in. I laid him out nicely, saluted, then buried him. Hopefully I'd never see him again.

My work done, I gathered my things, shovel included as I just knew I'd need it, and with the map secured in my pocket I left that place, vowing never to return.

Off We Go

I secured the shovel across my back like a gunslinger, using the straps of my backpack to hold it in place. Then I filled my water bottles from the well at the base of the cliff, thankful it still offered up its crisp, mineral-rich succor. The water was why the village was here, and had even been piped up to the caves but must have clogged over the years.

With a final glance at the village, I set off into the desert like I had before, except this time I knew exactly what I was doing, where I was going. Which, quite frankly, made it much worse. I knew what to expect, and none of it was good. First a quick detour to the truck to get the rest of my gear, then the adventure would truly begin.

Ten minutes later I was regretting not taking this trip at night. The day was blistering even by Ethiopian standards. The sun was fierce, as though angry with me for something, and the shade offered by Grace did little to help. Even the magic that swirled around my head and cooled my overheating brain wasn't up to such a challenge and soon it faltered completely.

Heat intensified. I regretted not wearing shorts but what self-respecting wizard would ever do that? My pack grew heavier by the minute.

I also got sand in my boots, in my mouth, and in crevices where I knew it would remain for years to come no matter what I did. So with my bits chafing, my lips already cracking, and the craving for a coffee and a nice breakfast gnawing at my insides, I waded through the dunes until I topped the rise. True desert lay before me in all its uncaring glory.

I headed into the west with the sun at my back, off on a fool's errand looking for who knew what.

Tired Already

There's a technique to walking in the desert. If you don't get it perfect, if you go out of the rhythm and lose the special swing of your hips, the ever so slight lift of the legs, almost gliding your feet across the sand as you put one foot slowly in front of the other whilst ensuring your boot lands flat for maximum surface area, then you are in for a very sorry time.

I could never figure out how to do it.

Nomads, and the many tribes of the desert, had this special way of walking down to a fine art. They almost floated across the dunes, having learned the hard way that unless you conserved every ounce of your energy you would be taken by the vastness and never return to your home and loved ones.

I had been shown many times by an increasingly exasperated Zewedu how to move in this particular fashion but could never quite get it to work.

What I ended up with was something unique to me, a way of walking that didn't utterly exhaust me but wasn't quite how you were meant to do things. Main thing is, it worked to a degree. I kind of slid the tip of my boot across the surface to bring the foot forward, gently tickling the top grains of sand, then plonked it down flat. More effort than the experts, less than someone new to the desert.

It was still exhausting.

The desert will catch you unawares unless you remain ever-vigilant. You have to constantly check your surroundings, watch the ground in front of you, take note of the sun's position and keep your destination firmly in mind. Otherwise, you'll wander around in circles endlessly until you eventually die.

One moment the ground is compact, the next your feet sink in like quicksand, and if you break your stride, lose your momentum, it sucks at your energy and destroys you.

Not only is walking on the flat treacherous in itself, with small pockets of cracked earth hidden beneath a dusting of sand waiting to twist your ankle and leave you hobbling about, but the moment you find yourself on even the slightest rise, on sand blown into almost imperceptible dunes by the fierce winds that scour the landscape clean, you become drained within minutes.

Walking on sand is like walking through snow, but a lot more tiring and you don't even get to go sledding. Your feet don't function properly and you find your body playing tricks on you, making the experience like wading through water. So, um, like snow and water then.

So, all of this is to say, that as I trudged across the barren desert, went up rises and down shallow banks, trod cracked earth and ground as soft as a bed of feathers, I was truly knackered and I'd only been walking for an hour.

The sun beat down on my back, Grace worked overtime to circulate cool air that simply wasn't enough to stop me perspiring heavily, and the silence, the utter quiet apart from the occasional call of a bird high above that glided past effortlessly, began to get to me.

I was in the zone now, at one with the desert and all it had to offer, all it had to take away. A man who belonged but who never truly belonged. It was like meeting an old friend again, someone you disliked but were drawn to nonetheless. Whose company you enjoyed but also hated because they were stronger than you, unyielding, stoic, old, and utterly set in their ways.

That's what the desert is like. An old, stubborn man whose been the same way for an age and isn't about to change now just to make your life easier.

You either accept this or you perish.

I learned it decades ago and I hadn't forgotten, which was probably why I hated, loathed with a passion, yet adored this barren place where there was nowhere to hide and the true essence of a man is laid bare. Such emptiness, being so alone, such hardship, it's a true test of your mettle. I wandered this place for many weeks, and I survived it. Sure, I wasn't in the best shape when I finally made my way to the city and the sanctuary of the Oasis, but I'd done better than most and beat the desert. Just.

But now, many years later, much older, maybe a little wiser or maybe a lot more foolish, I was faltering after a mere hour.

I told myself it was just that I needed to acclimatize. I wasn't used to the heat, the silence, the space, but I knew it was more than that. This was no place for me now, I no longer belonged. I was a foreign invader and I felt it in my bones that the desert would test me to see if I was welcome again. I would survive or be destroyed, no middle ground.

Which kinda sucked because I had a long way to go and I knew that once I arrived at my destination things would only get worse.

Closing In

I cursed Zewedu as I trudged over shallow dunes that in no way helped my progress. I drank water but was constantly parched. I checked the map repeatedly, scanning in all directions to ensure I was heading the right way.

A compass would have been nice, just for a sense of security, but I shouldn't second-guess myself. My inner compass had never let me down yet, even under such extreme conditions.

What I really wished I had was a portable freezer large enough for me to curl up inside. Multiple times, I considered using magic to cool my system down but I knew I had to watch myself, that this was merely the beginning of whatever adventure I was to be led on, and a little discomfort should have been the least of my worries. Still, it was bloody hot.

Sand worked its way into my boots and then through my socks. My big toe began to chafe and I knew I'd have the mother of all blisters soon enough.

Hunger grew, visions of sausages and runny fried eggs kept crowding my head, making me lose focus and mistime my steps. I shook away such stupid thoughts, reminding myself that I'd only been walking a few hours and this was nothing, a mere stroll.

I stopped and checked the map once more, happy, and surprised, to find I was mere minutes from my destination if my map-reading skills were still as good as they used to be.

The landscape was utterly barren here, the dunes giving way to a flat expanse that extended as far as I could see in all directions. I moved carefully going down the last dune and then was on parched earth where no rain had fallen for many years. Nothing grew here, no weeds, no grass, not a hint of anything green.

But off in the distance, shimmering in the heat haze, was what appeared to be a stunted tree, long dead, with jagged branches presumably as desiccated as Zewedu's skin. I headed towards the lone landmark, knowing this would be where he'd marked X on his damn map.

The tree was about ten feet tall, the main trunk split into three at waist height. Branches spread from the boughs, snapped off and brittle. Twigs littered the ground.

I hoisted myself up and sat in the crook of the tree to rest and steal what little shade the branches offered, which was minimal, but you take what you can get in such circumstances. There was nothing else around, not a soul to be seen, and even the birds had flown off to take shelter from the blazing sun.

After a drink and a battle with mental images of sizzling sausages, I reluctantly dropped to the ground and searched for clues.

Why had the map sent me here? Why had Zewedu wanted me to follow this ridiculous treasure trail? What was the point? When could I go home? Should I? Should I just pack this all in now before I got any deeper down the rabbit hole? Go home to my family and refuse to let Zewedu reach out to me like this from beyond the grave and screw with me?

I wished I could, but I couldn't. Part of it was that I understood this was unfinished business somehow, that my old master had one last lesson to teach me, one more thing to show me, but to be honest not even the thought of his disembodied head pestering me until my last breath was the reason I didn't just hightail it out of there and go get a sandwich. It was pure nosiness. My inquisitive nature wouldn't let me leave. I wanted to know what all the fuss was about, what was hidden here. Maybe it was a cool artifact, maybe it was a secret spell written long ago by my master and only now did he feel I was ready for such power.

Maybe it was his toe nail clippings. I wouldn't put it past the old bastard. He'd be there in Hades, cackling as he watched me suffer for nothing.

But maybe, just maybe, it was something super cool and I'd regret it forever if I let the opportunity pass me by.

So I unhitched my backpack, took a gulp of water, and began to dig.

Fed Up

Fifteen minutes later, I was down to my boots and boxer shorts. Slathered in sunscreen, I was oiled up to the max, slick with sweat, the salt stinging my eyes, and sand was stuck everywhere. I got the sneaking suspicion that sunscreen wasn't designed for such extremes and the sweat was probably making it run, at least judging by the white streaks. Not wanting to risk being burned alive, I cast a silent spell and felt my will swirl sluggishly around my body before my skin tingled as magic upped my defenses and would save me from becoming a lobster in the next few seconds.

It was a waste, but extreme sunburn is a killer, not to mention the heatstroke I knew I was already close to suffering. With my skin tingling, sweat dripping, and sunscreen running down my thighs, this poor old wizard in his old leather boots, his hat, and not much else resumed digging around the base of a dead tree, looking for treasure in the African desert.

All I found was more sand.

Between rests that grew longer than the actual digging time, I dug away until the sun rose high and I'd made a trench in a semi-circle. Then I had to stop because I may have been slightly deranged but I wasn't insane enough to dig in that kind of heat. I rested up in the tree and draped my jacket over the branches giving me the first genuine shade of the day and making me question why I hadn't done this before I commenced digging.

Lunch time came and went, the heat grew until I swear the sand itself began to sweat, and I sat there, unmoving, sweat sticking me to the dry wood, as I waited out the day until I could resume my work.

Strange insects wandered around the ground, investigating the hole I'd made, sliding down the sides then clambering up and out once they realized there was nothing of interest.

Soon I was lost to daydreams of the past again, of when I was young, but they were bad memories, full of sadness and despair, of true hunger as my parents left me to fend for myself if I could scrape together enough money for some basic food. They were such bad people, no wonder I left as soon as I could. No wonder I did what I did to them yet remained in that apartment alone with them for weeks even after they were dead, until the day I figured out what to do with them. I'd finally removed any trace of their deaths before leaving, never to return.

Nobody ever missed them, or me, and just like that we were gone. I had a new start, a chance at a future. To live it in any way I saw fit without them slowly killing me day by day with their utter lack of interest.

Ugh, long time ago, different life. I was a man now and had made my life something worth living no thanks to them. Why think of them now? It was the desert, the emptiness, it sent you back in time to relive old memories. The desert opens you up and reveals the truth about the person you are, and you better be sure you can live with what you find as it has no mercy, holds no quarter. I could handle it, I didn't regret what I did to them, only what they did to me.

The day passed like a dream. Afternoon morphed into evening and the desert began to cool.

Guess the rest was over. Time to dig.

Again.

Some Company

You don't get long, languid sunrises and sunsets in the desert. It's more like somebody turns a powerful light switch on or off.

One minute it was twilight, the next the desert was plunged into darkness. Night comes early and is total.

I placed the portable lights at the base of the tree then cursed my ineptitude for not gathering up the dried wood and making a fire. Wanting to resume my work, but nonetheless knowing it was sensible not only for warmth but to deter predators, I gathered up every scrap of firewood, resisted breaking branches off the dead tree, then made myself a compact yet very comforting fire far enough away so the tree didn't go up in flames but close enough so I could feel its warmth.

For added light, and even more security, I stuck a protesting Wand in the ground. He shone like a beacon, a pure white light that cast strange shadows from the tree like a man with misshapen limbs.

Now I could dig.

With the fire crackling, Wand complaining, and darkness held at bay for a while, I felt almost normal, like I was back home and out in the fields having a fire and readying for barbecue. My stomach rumbled. Not quite the same as being at home then. I couldn't pop inside to raid the fridge and there was certainly no ketchup.

The work continued at a decent pace. It was cool enough to feel good moving, the action of digging keeping me warm without fear of overheating. That isn't to say it didn't get bloody tedious, because it did. My arms ached, my shoulders were sore, my back was in half, and I cursed Zewedu repeatedly. Around I went in a circle, finishing off the trench until I created a miniature moat circling the tree.

I found nothing.

How far away from the tree should I dig? How deep to go? There were no instructions, just the map with the bloody X. A large shape drawn right by the tree, assuming I was even in the right place. I thought I was, but it was a big desert and a little map so would be easy to be off by a large margin.

As I stood back to admire my handiwork and consider my next step, something clicked in my head and I examined the map again. I positioned myself so I had the points of the compass lined up with the map and then grabbed a stick and drew a literal X on the ground in the exact same position as on the map.

"You would, wouldn't you?" I muttered to the memory of my master. "You always were a literal bugger, so I guess when you draw an X you mean dig an X. Okay, you old goat, you win, I'll do it your way."

With a new plan, maybe even a little hope this would soon be over, I resumed my work.

It wasn't long before the firewood was exhausted, me along with it. I paused and stepped closer to the dying fire to take what warmth I could.

Sounds of the desert grew intense, the animals on the roam, sensible enough to lay low during the heat and venture forth at night. Howls, barks, the call of birds, all shattered the silence that had descended when the day was first vanished.

I became alert as something approached, an animal treading carefully but unable to mask its movements from a trained wizard. I'd learned to become attuned to the slightest sound out here, you had to if you wanted to survive. Animals would attack, constantly hungry and on the lookout for sustenance, and you couldn't blame them but you had to look out for number one.

It paused just out of sight. Some creatures would tear right in and take their chances, others were more cautious, merely drawn to the noise, unlikely to attack something much larger than themselves. But you never knew and it's a scary business. You feel alone, defenseless, at their mercy even though I knew I could take care of myself. It's the element of surprise most carnivores rely on, they lay in wait then when they see an opportunity they take it and pounce, tear into your belly and then you're a late supper.

With the cold biting, I ignored the watcher and continued digging along the lines of the X shallowly so it was marked out before I dug deep.

I glanced up as I sensed the creature had come closer and was surprised and shocked to note it was an Ethiopian wolf. They were very rare now, almost driven to extinction, so to see one was a treat indeed. Almost like a fox in shape and gait, it sat beside the embers of the fire and cocked its head as it stared at me, probably wondering what the mad dude was doing out here in the middle of nowhere. I wondered the same thing.

Its ears twitched as it took in the scene, then it appeared satisfied and scratched at an ear, doing that comical thing dogs do and looking like it was smiling. Maybe it was. Laughing, more like.

"Yeah, I know. Hilarious."

And so I dug while my companion for the evening sat and watched. I looked up much later to find him curled up with his head resting on a paw. He opened an eye and glanced at me warily, checking we were cool.

"Don't you worry about a thing, friend, you're safe here with me."

He blinked then curled up tighter and closed his eyes. He let out a groan then sighed and began to snore quietly, a background hum to the desert that was somehow soothing, as though he was saying everything would work out fine in the end.

I had my doubts about that, but what did I know?

Getting Ridiculous

I dug, I rested, I dug some more.

The wolf slept, the wolf snored, the wolf was lucky.

At some point during the night, when I was utterly spent, I must have stumbled over to the embers and curled up beside the lucky fella, although I have no recollection. I awoke with a start and stared at the moon, cold, confused, and aching more than I'd believed possible.

My new companion opened a lazy eye then went back to sleep. Guess I wasn't as intimidating as I'd imagined.

Reluctantly, I clambered to my feet and shook out the stiffness in my joints. And then I got back to work, knowing if I put it off much longer I'd be back to another blistering day with nothing to show for it but a trench.

Rested, the work moved at a good pace and soon I'd got down several spades deep along the arms of the

X. I moved to where the lines bisected and slammed the spade into the ground.

The metal sliced in deep and easy then kept going like I'd hit an air pocket. I pulled out the shovel and with it came a noxious smell. I jumped back, concerned it could be deadly. Gas trapped beneath the earth for who knew how long could be poisonous or flammable, easily knock me out then kill me where I lay. Yes, I was becoming paranoid.

The ground hissed. I grabbed Wand and shook him to life so I could see what was happening. There was a pit, the ground sinking around the perimeter. How deep was the pocket of emptiness? I took a step away as the hole deepened and spread wider. Sand and pebbles fell into blackness, the ripples stretching as wide as my arms, the smell increasing, malodorous and toxic.

With a whine, the wolf stood and craned its head forward. He took a tentative sniff, then barked before growling at the spreading hole. My new buddy glanced at me and one ear with a distinct white marking twitched, then he took off into the night.

"See ya," I said, sad to see my friend go.

Several seconds later I heard him howl in the distance, probably telling me to scarper too. I wasn't that sensible.

As if to prove that point, the ground vibrated, I took several hurried steps back, but the hole expanded and the ground rippled then tilted sideways as if I was on a boat in a storm, and the next thing I knew I was falling.

I landed on my arse and frantically tried to grip onto the sides of the steep banks as I slid down into the depths of the earth. The stench intensified as I sank lower, scrabbling and clawing in a desperate attempt to remain above ground.

Wand vibrated and nonchalantly said, "Dig me into the ground, I'll hold us in place," but I just scowled at him as what use was that when the ground was falling anyway?

"Any other bright ideas?" I asked.

"Um, run?" he offered.

"Not helping."

It was too late anyway. The angle sharpened, the hole widened. I was catapulted into the center of emptiness and plummeted into a very uncertain future.

Magic Cushion

Certain it would hurt unless I acted quickly, I let my will surge, tensed my buttocks and anything else I could, even though it all ached, and drew in the very air around me to act as a buffer to my inevitable meeting with the ground.

Just in time, I landed with a jolt, the tightly packed air molecules acting like an uncomfortable cushion that nonetheless knocked the wind out of me but left me with all bones intact if somewhat rattly.

Wand emitted a powerful light. I got the distinct impression it was as much for himself as me, but said nothing as I didn't want to hurt his feelings. With my stiff buddy held aloft, dirt falling on my hat and drumming my brain, I stepped to the side to get some respite and check out the cavern, cave, or whatever it was.

Guess I'd found what Zewedu wanted me to find, but I wish he'd given me a heads-up. He'd be loving this, the old trickster.

Not wanting to get a face full of grit, but risking it nonetheless, I looked up once I was well away from the worst of the landfall. I saw stars through a hole probably six feet wide although it was hard to tell. I guess I was a good thirty feet underground at least, and knew there was no way I could climb out from something so deep even if I had a bloody ladder. Okay, I'd sure try if I did, but I didn't, and I had no Teleron or anything of that nature that could get me out of here without a struggle.

I turned my attention to my more immediate surroundings. It was cave-like, just as I expected. Solid rock walls impossible to climb and compact ground with a soft mound in the center where I'd fallen in.

What was this place? What was its purpose? When was dinner?

Time for a tour. If there was a way in, if Zewedu knew about this place, then there had to be a way out. If the slippery snake had entered, he'd left too, and if he could do it then so could I. No way was I gonna let him beat me, ruin me, not when I had so much to lose for the first time in my life.

Gingerly, I walked the perimeter, shining Wand on the rough walls. In places there were signs of the cave being at least partially man made, with marks where the stone had been hacked at, small recesses made and traces of old tallow and wax used to light the space.

I'd heard of places like this, used in a similar fashion to the houses in the mountain. Somewhere to keep cool during the heat of the day, somewhere safe, away from predators, but more often used for much darker purposes. Not the norm for citizens but for the practitioners of dark arts that often holed up for months, sometimes years, in the desert to hone their skills and get in touch with various nasties from the Nolands. I never touched the dark stuff, it left all who dabbled with it bitter, twisted, ruined, and dangerous. Dark magic is a real thing, true sinister stuff, a bottomless pit of power that can be tapped into the same as I used magic, but it comes at a terrible price, taking with it your sanity and any sense of morality as your power increases.

Nobody who immersed themselves in such forces ever emerged the same. There were true terrors lurking and it wormed its way inside your head, gnawed away at the goodness, and left you stark, raving mad, and utterly evil.

With my thoughts suitably pessimistic, and with visions of nasties right this moment amassing to do something despicable when they burst through the thin veil between this world and theirs, I shivered but continued my search.

Wonder what I'd find? Maybe Zewedu had left me something nice after all this trouble.

I found it. It wasn't nice.

That Feeling

You know that feeling you get when you're sure something bad is about to happen but you don't know what?

I'd had that ever since I set foot in this strange land again, but it paled into insignificance as a smell I'd almost forgotten sent my nose to twitching and me wishing I had a handkerchief. It took several fraught seconds for my brain to catch up with what my body was telling me, and then I felt true dread as I put the pieces of the puzzle together.

Like the sucker for punishment I was, I turned back to the rock and stretched Wand out as far as I could reach. It was as though the walls were alive, squirming and moving, pulsing with slow, agonizing life.

But it wasn't life, it was much worse.

It was death.

They're Real All Right

"Fuck," seemed the most appropriate response.

I danced back hurriedly, almost tripped on the loose dirt in the center of the cavern, but somehow remained upright as I moved as far away as I could from the blasphemous sight. The milky whites of their eyes glistened as Wand's light was reflected from the unseeing orbs, the creatures acting on instinct, scent, or the mere magic that animated their corpses.

There were no sudden movements. No lunges, no shouts of "Brains," just slow, wobbly, almost jelly-like twitching of limbs as the dead came to temporary life and moved towards the source of their awakening.

Me.

Yeah, that's right.

Zombies!

Kind of. Okay, not really, just the animated corpses of almost-dead practitioners. Brought back to life by stagnant magic trapped underground, created long ago by a group of utter halfwits who thought it would be fun to venture onto the other side but leave their bodies behind to be re-animated when they felt the time was right. And the right time was when someone full of magic came to visit and they could suck the magical juices out of him and get a second chance at life.

So, um, yeah, I guess they were zombies of a sort, just not your regular brain-munchers. Something much more worrying.

Half-dead wizards. Quite a few by the looks of it.

The room was lit up like midday as Wand increased the intensity.

"Gee, thanks, just what I wanted," I moaned, getting the full-effect of the not-at-all-recently dead.

"Thought it would help. You know, for the blasting," said Wand with more glee than I felt was warranted.

"Ace, can't wait." I had visions of being splattered with crusty old wizard goo but such is the life of a downtrodden wizard at times.

There were five of them, all naked, all leathery dark skin like Zewedu, all just as dead until a moment ago. But not quite. These guys went into something akin to death-limbo as their spirits departed. Their immersion in dark magic allowing them to remove the shackles of mortality and travel in spirit to regions they could never truly return from. What they left behind was enough of a spark to bring them back at least in part, for their bodies to remain almost, but not quite corpses. For all intents and purposes they had been dead and still were, a bit.

Vague? Yes. About as much as I knew? Absolutely.

Worrying? You betcha.

The corpses eased away from the wall slowly, focused on me and the mighty Wand — a beacon of hope where otherwise all would be darkness. They sensed the power, wanted to feed on it. Couldn't wait to stuff their faces and feast on pure magic that would draw them back to this realm and let them do more nasty stuff to themselves because they were addicts same as me.

No chance. I would not go out like this, being devoured by a bunch of dead dudes in a cave far from home. I was going to die at home, in bed, preferably after a nice cuppa and a biscuit or three. Ones with chocolate on.

As they closed in, so they became increasingly animated, buoyed by the magic. I felt their power, felt them reach for the magic in the air and draw it inside themselves, becoming stronger by the second. One reached a shaky hand forward, the nails hard and long like talons. Their faces were gaunt, the cheekbones almost piercing taut skin that looked hundreds of years old. And the eyes, oh the eyes. Filled with torment and the madness of ages, their spirits trapped forever in a terrible realm where the only escape was insanity.

If they returned they would be utterly corrupt, impossibly mad, and all the more dangerous for it. I could just imagine a horde of zombie wizards running amok in the desert, terrifying the local villagers and hurting the innocent. For this is what they thrived on, innocence and purity, using it to entrench themselves more deeply than ever in all that was bad in the world.

The lead dude reached for Wand, his hand closing surprisingly fast, but we were ready for him, and the rest. Energy shot down my arm and into my friend, powering him up to the max. Sigils flared in a blurry sequence along his shaft, glowing purple and green just for the effect, and then we lit up that cruel cavern like it was New Year's Eve.

Magic popped and hissed, crackled and exploded like no expense was spared for the display, and as the undead were drawn to the light show so it morphed into something much more deadly. Bright light became dark, then less than nothing as the cavern was plunged into utter darkness.

There was no sound, not even a moan, no raspy breathing, no motion save me and Wand as we did what we did best. Killed bad guys.

The magic worked as it was designed to, the pockets of emptiness would already have found their targets and be devouring anything in their path. Once I felt the work was in full-effect, Wand lit up the room just for the comfort as much as to witness the magic in operation.

To be fair, it wasn't really a fight so much as a disposal job of trash long overdue being taken out. The corpses still stood, no motion now, just open-mouthed carapaces that became less and less as I watched. Dark patches spread across torsos and limbs as ancient flesh and bone was devoured, and when the legs were eaten away so the bodies tumbled to the ground and there they remained.

There were no cries, no wild flapping of arms, no protestations. They merely ceased to be, and for good this time. I allowed the spell to wane, the life force truly gone from these men who would pervert magic and had hoped to cross a boundary that should never be crossed. Guess the same could be said of me, but I was still the good guy. At least I hoped I was.

"What next, Zewedu, a pit of vipers?" No sooner had the words left my lips than I clamped a had over my mouth and stared into the shadows, hoping like hell no snakes appeared.

None did. Neither did anything else.

A Waiting Game

I expected more of the same, for it to be an escalation of madness until I didn't know what I was doing or what my name was. It was something much worse. Nothing at all. Just me, Wand, and what remained of the dead dudes.

I performed a very, and I mean very, thorough search of the cavern but found no interesting artifacts, no more corpses, and no way out. There had to be, I knew there did, but I searched in vain and discovered nothing that even hinted at a secret door or even a coil of rope. But I knew Zewedu. If he'd found this place then he sure as shit didn't climb back out the way he'd got in, if he even came down the way I had.

After a fruitless hour I was utterly beat. Magic was low, energy was depleted, and the digging, the hunger, and the sheer shock of being back here all conspired to leave me at my lowest point for many a year.

Cold took hold. Not the biting cold of up above in the desert, but enough to leave me chilled through and in need of warmth. What to burn though? There was no wood, no means of getting any at this point, and rocks aren't known for their ability to combust. I glanced over at the corpses.

No, I couldn't. Could I?

Yes, I could actually, for a wizard in need is a wizard indeed, and I was indeed a wizard with a need. Knowing it was all I had left to give and then I'd be tapped out, I got close to the guys and let Wand work our final magic of the day. He poured my waning energy all over them, dried them out until they truly were husks. The meat became something else, the bone likewise. What normally happens over aeons happened in ten minutes of focused effort. They became a different form of carbon. Like brittle coal that would see me through the night if I didn't think about what I was burning.

The bodies crumbled before my eyes until there was no way to tell they were once human beings. I bid them a final farewell as I built myself a nice bonfire that left me sweating. The flames banished the shadows with their light, and I rested, smiling, knowing that such a cremation was all they deserved. At least they finally became useful, as I doubted they were ever of any help when alive.

I slept the sleep of the victorious, and didn't have a single bad dream.

My Prize

When I awoke in the morning, I was stiffer than Wand. Everything hurt, including things I hadn't known were mine until now. Aches merged to create an all-over pain that burrowed deep into my bones and left me raw, utterly sapped of energy. I also had a deep hunger I wasn't sure I could ever satisfy.

I groaned as I shifted on the ground, as that's what wizards do in the morning whether they're suffering or not, but somehow managed to get into a sitting position.

The wizard fire was still burning, the smoke drifted up lazily to the clear blue sky above, and to be honest the smell was less than favorable. It was downright noxious in fact.

Unable to stand it any longer, I spread the coals, a stupid idea as it billowed with smoke and dust, leaving me spluttering and cursing, something I also often did in the morning, usually after looking in the mirror. I kicked against a hard piece of what I assumed was desiccated evil wizard but it didn't break up. With the toe of my boot I shifted it aside and then plonked myself back down with surprise. I sat and stared at a large ebony box, covered in ash, with what appeared to be brass inlay on the top in random decorative patterns typical of the region.

For some time I did nothing but sit and ponder, then I did a bit of speculating, and then proceeded to ignore it completely and scratch at my beard which felt like I'd collected half the Sahara in it. My tongue was swollen and dry, my lips were cracked, my eyelids were gritty, and my nose was blocked with dry bits of nasty wizard particles.

I really needed a shower, and to brush my teeth.

Ah, yes, that's what I'd do. I rummaged around in my pack and retrieved my toiletry bag then gave my teeth a lovely long brush. It in no way made me feel better, but it sure didn't make me feel any worse. Now I just felt like utter crap but with nice clean teeth.

Ablutions over, if not complete, and with no need for a pee as I was too dried up inside, I sat back down, crossed my legs, and waited for something to happen, as this time I was certain something would.

There I remained for a day, and then a freezing cold night, and then another day.

At least it was quiet, and I was out of the worst of the heat, but a TV would have been nice, food even nicer.

A Question of Motive

Why didn't I just grab the damn box and open it immediately? Good question, and one I asked myself many times as I sat waiting. Partly because I didn't trust Zewedu, but the main reason was because for once I wasn't sure I wanted more adventure.

If I opened it there would be no closing it. Whatever waited inside would lead me to places I wouldn't want to go, and do things I wouldn't want to do. There was no way I had been dragged all this way for something petty. Look what had happened already and the fun and games hadn't even begun yet. What would this lead to? Where would it take me? Would there be biscuits?

So I sat, and I glowered, and I glared, and I grumbled, and I became lost to a peculiar kind of madness. Visions came unbidden, mixed with memories of the past, of places and faces I didn't care to recall. Lights burned my retinas, pains stabbed my body, but it was all in my head, brought on by lack of food and no water for the last day.

I became delirious, believed I had already opened the box and found it empty. At one point, I truly believed I was walking the desert, but came to with a bump on my head as I walked straight into the wall of my prison.

But everything passes, and there came a time when I knew I could hold out no longer.

Crunch time.

Either open it up and take the consequences, or leave it well alone and figure out how to escape this cell of stone and death.

Guess which one I chose.

Shocker

I snatched up the box and without preamble opened the lid. Whatever happened would just have to do its worst. No, I wasn't prepared, very ill-prepared in fact. All I had was magic topped up as much as it could be under the circumstances, which was pretty good but I wasn't at full throttle with such low energy reserves.

Expecting the worst, I winced and turned away, but nothing tried to bite my face off, no magic emanated from within, there were no wards protecting the contents, and no spells leaked out and began chewing away at my brain.

Relieved, I risked a quick glance then looked away immediately, just in case it was activated by sight.

Several seconds later, my mind registered what my eyes had seen and I clutched the box tight then sat back down and took a proper look.

It couldn't be, could it? Where would Zewedu get such a thing? How could he get it? Did it even exist? Guess it did, and this was confirmation.

What did I do now? Could I close the lid and forget this had ever happened? No chance. The cat was well and truly out of the bag now.

"You've really done it this time, Zewedu," I croaked, my throat so raw it came out as a whisper.

My old master's head appeared in the gloom, eyes wide, the orbs threaded with veins, the rheumy whites like moldy custard. Tears fell from the corners and his mouth stretched, ready for him to scream at me once more.

But he didn't scream, he did something even more unnerving.

He smiled.

And then he was gone.

"Farewell, for the last time," I whispered, for I knew he was finally at peace.

I never saw him again.

Figuring Stuff Out

I had to get a move on. Every wizard, adept, chaser of artifacts, nutjob, wannabe, and freak in the world would hear about this soon enough, and many would already be aware that such a prize had been uncovered. Wizards have a sixth sense for special artifacts, can sniff them out, find their way directly to them.

And this was the biggie, the main one, the be-all and end-all of artifacts. This was where it all began, what it was all about. The big kahuna.

And I had it, more's the pity.

Time to get my skates on and escape this hole.

Only problem being, I didn't know how to.

Which was an issue.

I was a sitting duck down here and this was no place to do battle with those who were on their way.

I sat down and gave it some thought. Which took a while.

No Choice

"You aren't going to like this," I told Wand.

"I'm hating it already. Isn't there another way?"

"If you can think of one, I'm all ears."

"Well," mused Wand, "they do stick out a lot, but I wouldn't say *all* ears."

"At least I have ears. Anyway, you ready?"

"No, but do I have a choice?"

"You do not." I slammed Wand's base into the rock and wiggled him about to create a decent-sized hole. Satisfied, I pulled him out and repeated the process as far up as I could reach.

Now, wood from the unicorn tree is incredibly hard, and once that wood becomes a wand, in this case, Wand, it takes on so much power it becomes almost indestructible. Hard as steel, tougher than this crumbly rock for sure, and with a little magic imbued in the shaft and tightly focused, he did an excellent impression of a pick.

I still had to climb though, and that would be an issue.

Nevertheless, with the ebony box in my pack, I jammed Wand in hard, bent my leg and found the toehold, then began the arduous climb to freedom.

It went rather well. I only fell seven times, only scraped one knee to the bone, Wand only complained a gazillion times, and in half an hour I emerged from the pit, crawled across the ground, got myself up in the tree, put up my jacket for shade, and promptly fell fast asleep.

Feed Me

I awoke with the mother of all headaches and a thirst that had to be quenched. The sun beat down with its usual intensity, and I could not stand it for a moment longer.

Knowing I had no choice, I dropped down and slowly trudged back to the village and the only water supply I knew of. Once I'd finally made it and drank until my belly was ready to burst, I filled up the bottles, stripped naked, and had the best wash of my life.

The water was cool and fresher than new underwear from Marks and Spencer. As I sluiced it over my body, the combustible wizard ash soaked into the sand and I felt alive in a spectacular way. This was what it was all about, getting back to basics, a man alone in the wild, testing his mettle, escaping from big holes, and going on quests.

My skin tingled and goosebumps rose as I stood in the shade and continued to pour life-giving water over my head until my scalp was numb.

A desert rabbit darted out from a hidey-hole in the rock, probably disturbed by my singing as most creatures, human and animal alike, usually are, and I grabbed a rock quickly and threw it. I hit my target dead-center.

Things were looking up. I had water, I had food, but I guess I should have some veggies too. Ah well, my five a day would have to wait for a while.

Still naked, I built myself a fire in the shade and feasted on stringy rabbit. It tasted amazing. I packed up what remained and stored it safely in my backpack then gave my clothes a thorough soaking before dressing with them still sopping wet.

With the light fading, I gathered more wood then built up a huge fire. By the time I was finished my clothes were dry, and just in time.

The desert cooled, the sun did its rapid disappearing act, and I rested my back against the rock and slept the sleep of the soon-to-be-thoroughly-annoyed. But for now, for a little while, I enjoyed the sounds of the desert and slept, unmolested, full of belly and empty of mind, satisfied I had put Zewedu to rest.

Another Day

In the morning, after brushing my teeth and even having a pee, I decided to save the rabbit and break my fast with more water. I used my water bottles to wash, then filled them up for the trip.

As the sun rose, I once more set off into the desert, heading back the way I'd come, where I'd pass the car and could then slowly make my way towards civilization.

Signs of my passing were eradicated by wind and sand, but I knew the way, no worries about getting lost. I moved at a decent pace, got into the rhythm and walked in a flow state, mind empty, focused yet not focused, merely put one foot in front of the other and refused to think about what I'd discovered.

Time enough for that later.

At some point I had a bit of a profound thought, or maybe just a regular one, and put up a deep, impenetrable ward around the box, masking it from prying magical eyes and doing what I could to hide the power I knew it was emitting to those searching the correct magical wavelengths. It wouldn't hide its location entirely, but it would make it impossible to pinpoint. Give me a fighting chance if, or when, anyone came hunting.

Job done, I continued, and eventually made it to the car. I dared not open the doors for fear of the heat that had built up inside, but underneath the truck was beautiful shade and I took full advantage and lay down prone, pulled Grace over my eyes, and slept out the worst of the heat.

I was rudely awakened by being dragged by my ankles, which is no way to wake up. Startled, I tried to sit up, and whacked my head so damn hard I saw stars. Out from under, and miffed, I kicked and squirmed until whoever was abusing me released their hold and I shot up to my feet, Wand already released, and sigils flared.

Somewhat cleverly, I was plunged into darkness as someone stuffed an old sack that smelled like it was used to carry rotten potatoes over my head then whacked in the spots at the back of my knees so I collapsed. I was booted in the ribs and as I keeled over forward I puked up in the bag as I was kicked in my man bits by someone with excellent aim and incredible leg power.

There are better ways to wake up, although at least this one was memorable.

Aha

The jokers hadn't done their homework, as making wizards puke up in stinky bags ain't any way to get them on your side. They'd also not considered Wand.

Even before my nose split, which it did a moment later as I dove headfirst into the dust, Wand was channeling my will in a rather volatile and undirected manner. I waved him left to right as I hit hard, searing a path in front of me at about shin height.

A man screamed blue murder and I heard him collapse, which you would if your legs have been detached from your body.

The person behind me shouted in a panic, so I rolled over, got a face full of puke, and repeated the action as Wand pulsed with glee. I heard a satisfying squelch as the dude's innards splashed onto the ground.

Warmth spread over my lower legs, and if I wasn't already utterly grossed out by my own vomit I probably would have puked again.

With my free hand I yanked the sack from my head, smearing sick through my hair and all over Grace, and took a fighting stance, ready to deal with anyone else. A quick spin and I was satisfied there was nobody else, so I took a look at the my less than worthy foe, once I'd cleared my face of half-digested rabbit bits.

The man who had sneaked up behind me was dead, his insides already drying, long sausages that would begin to sizzle soon enough.

The other one was alive, legs severed halfway up his shins, and he was shaking terribly as he stared at his feet off to the side laying there like props. They looked fake, like a bad imitation of real feet, dirty and with chipped toenails. Flies were already feasting on the warm blood.

"Who are you?" I asked, not unkindly as he was in a bit of a bad way. Then I recalled he'd kicked me in the knackers so I grabbed him and shook him back to reality.

He spoke in a local dialect so I repeated my question in loud English so he'd understand as that's what you do when abroad, but he shook his head, his eyes rolled up in their sockets, and he died.

Unable to think with all the gunk over my face, I rapidly stripped and cleaned myself up best I could. I'd never get rid of the smell, it would linger forever, but I did what I could.

With my water wasted, I searched the bodies but there was nothing to find. Each man wore nothing but a pair of thin cotton trousers, a lightweight shirt, and had a small bag containing water, some dried fruit, and their staffs which lay next to them where they died.

Local wizards, not powerful, but close enough to feel the call from the artifact. The first of many, no doubt, but they'd come close to getting me, and the box, so I had to be more cautious. No more sleeping under trucks for The Stinky Hat, I'd have to remain out in the open and vigilant from now on.

Time to up my game if I was ever to get out of the desert alive.

Over to the north was a rise then a dip, obscuring the desert, so I headed that way and was pleased I'd been right. Their vehicle was there, out of sight, and I guess it had been there for the night judging by the way the sand banked up on one side against the wheels.

I found the keys in the ignition, rummaged around in the truck bed and found more food, enough for days, and then I hopped in, started it up, and drove up onto the road, not quite believing my stroke of luck.

Apart from the sick thing, that was gross, and far from lucky.

Where To?

I whistled as I drove carefully along the dirt track, not wanting to risk damage to the battered vehicle, just happy to rest my weary bones.

It was slow going, but certainly faster than walking, and if nothing went wrong I could be back in Dire Dawa by the next day, home a few days later. Ah, home, it felt like a lifetime since I'd left, almost like it was all a dream. Did I really own all those things? Have a house, loads of stuff? Barns and more cars than I could recall, magic portals, artifacts, money? And two wonderful women to share it with? Surely that wasn't real? It felt so remote, like it was somebody else's life, not mine.

I ached to return to that life, to know comfort, to have a hug and to ogle my kitchen. Soon, I'd get there soon. I just had to remain vigilant, stay alive, and figure out what to do with this damn box.

What should I do?

This was too important to dismiss, and I couldn't even if I wanted to. Others were on the hunt as had just been made obvious, so I had to decide what to do. Maybe I should take some more time and beef the wards up further, do my utmost to hide the artifact inside from every being on the magical radar. No, I'd already done the best I could, the only thing to do was get home and think of a plan then.

For now I just had to keep hold of it, keep my hands off it, not be tempted, and try to forget the power I now held at my fingertips. I knew enough about this uber-artifact to know I should never use it, not even touch it, as it had driven many an adept to the far corners of madness because of what it could do.

So I drove, remained focused, and munched on fruit and dried meat I'd stolen from two wannabes who should have known better than to ever kick The Hat in the balls.

Everything still smelled of sick; guess I'd have to live with that.

Typical

About an hour into the journey, just as I felt I was getting somewhere, there appeared a sight familiar from my time here before. A large caravan of nomads were crossing the desert on their annual trading route. Passing numerous small villages and remote communities along the way, they traded, bartered, bought, and sold all manner of items to allow them to continue their way of life.

It was a sight to behold, and I had no choice but to stop and wait for the long train of camels, mules, men, women, and children to pass.

I turned off the engine and watched as camels laden with anything from pots and pans to handmade blankets, rugs, even small items of furniture, walked stoically past, giving me the indifferent look camels always did, disinterested and aloof, the same attitude as cats. Camels are perfect for the desert, a true hardy creature able to traverse the long distances between water holes without difficulty, providing strength, fuel when their dung was dried, and even meat if life got too hard.

I rested against the truck and watched the procession. Men and women wore brightly colored clothes made during the long days and nights they spent inside their tents, many wore jewelry of brass or silver, and they laughed and joked as they walked. They were happy, enjoyed this way of life even though they knew it was no longer the way things were. Even when I was here before, traditions had changed and the life had become harder as the villages they passed through grew smaller or were deserted entirely.

It became tough for them to sustain their traditions, more difficult to earn enough to continue their never-ending travels around the region, but they clung to the old ways and by the looks of it the numbers in this particular group had grown rather than dwindled.

Several young children, barefoot, wearing nothing but shorts, came running over to me, smiling and shoving each other forward to be the first to talk to the foreigner.

"Hey, little dudes, what you doing?"

They didn't understand, merely stared at me, wide-eyed and full of wonder as they fidgeted and whispered to each other. One of them said something to the others and they all ran off, screaming and laughing, back to their extended family.

The children ran up to a man and talked all at once, pointing over at me. I waved and the man waved back. He was tall, with short-cropped hair, and wore a traditional red and blue skirt type thing perfect for the weather and traveling long distances without discomfort.

He spoke to the children then approached me. His gait was a perfect example of how to move, and he almost glided across the parched earth.

I sensed a familiarity in his movements, his build, and a particular tilt of the head. But when he was close enough, it was the warm, open smile that left me in no doubt that I knew this man.

"Hello, my old friend," said Marcus, as he offered a hand.

"Marcus, you look the same as the day I left." I shook his hand, it was warm and calloused, the grip firm.

"And you look like you have been in the desert, my friend." Marcus smiled, knowing only too well what the desert can do to a man.

"A little detour. Unfinished business."

"Ah yes, you have returned to the village," he said knowingly, his accent so thick I had to focus hard to make out the words. Marcus had learned English when young, taught by his father, but when I met him he hadn't had much chance to practice as a young man similar in age to me, and I guess that hadn't changed. Also, why he was called Marcus still felt odd, as it certainly wasn't an Ethiopian name. But many parents called their children by two names, hoping that it would lead to wealth and all the trappings of a world that may just as well have been a million miles away from here.

"Yep, Zewedu called me. But that's done with now, demons have been put to rest."

"It has been so long, we were young boys when you departed. I see you made it through the desert, my friend."

"Sure did. Your hospitality helped, but I was still out there for many weeks after you left."

"It is beautiful, is it not? The desert makes you who you are."

"Sure is, and it sure did. So, you still traveling?"

"I will always travel, and now I have a family. We grow strong out here, our numbers multiply." As if on cue, the children came tearing back to us, braver now they had backup.

"Ah, my children," he said, beaming with pride.

"What, all of them?" I asked, counting six smiling little kids.

"Yes," he said, almost bursting. "And there is another one soon on its way. I am a lucky man."

"You sure are. Blessed."

"Come, my friend, you must eat with us. Tell your stories, you must have many tales to tell." Marcus put an arm around my shoulder.

"I do have a tale or two," I admitted.

"Then it is settled. You will spend the evening with us, sleep on a bed, and then tomorrow you can continue your journey."

With a shrug, I said, "Why not?" It would be nice to have company, hear about Marcus' life, and a bed sounded divine.

So I grabbed the keys and my pack and joined the procession as we headed off into the desert.

A Pleasant Evening

"And then the tentacled monster smashed through the glass and the acid water it lived in washed into the room and began to eat away the floor." The children gasped, oohed and aahed, their eyes wide. They huddled close to me, sat forward as I told my tale, another adventure for The Hat. It looked like Marcus' translation was adding even further embellishment to my tale.

Marcus smiled and nodded, happy to hear about my life and what I'd been up to. We'd already spoken over dinner, telling each other of our lives, and now most of the tribe, including all children from babes and up, were in the communal tent, a large fire in the center, and the stories were being told.

"And now it is time for bed," he said to me, before turning to the children and repeating it in the local dialect.

There were grumbles and groans but they did as they were told, and I was lucky enough to get a kiss from each cheeky child before their mothers took them off to the private tents to sleep.

Marcus and I moved to a spot by the fire and spoke in low tones well into the night about magic and monsters, family and friends, about people we'd lost, people we'd found, and how our lives had turned out after decades of maturing.

He was happy, content, had no interest in changing things. My friend was born into this life and loved it. He had a pretty wife who was heavily pregnant, his children, and his travels. What more could a man want? He had asked me that. It was a good question. But I enjoyed my life, one very different to his, and I realized I wouldn't change it for anything.

He showed me to a small tent with rolls of bedding. I said a thankful goodnight before I crept under the covers and slept a beautiful sleep that only the desert can bring about.

In the morning everything was bustle and busy, busy, busy. They had places to be, items to trade, and a timetable to keep. I helped dismantle the tents and pack everything up, and by the time the sun was becoming uncomfortable we had finished. We ate a light breakfast of bread and dried fruit then they were gone.

Marcus turned and waved before disappearing down the dunes.

It was good to see him, another old friend from the past.

Feeling great about life, I retraced my steps back to the truck, unsurprised to find somebody had nicked it.

I should have known I couldn't escape the desert so easily.

I Walk

Maybe it was because I was heading away from the grip of old memories, maybe it was because Zewedu was finally at rest and no longer pestering me, maybe it was because I knew I'd done what he wanted. Or maybe it was because of meeting Marcus. Whatever the reason, I was light of spirit as I walked along the dust track and headed to the village I'd got the truck from. It was quite a trek, and I had a ways to go, but I should arrive by evening if I maintained my pace and only rested for a few hours in the afternoon.

Then it was a trip to the city, then home. Woo-hoo, I couldn't wait.

The sun beat down, I munched on rabbit and other dried meats, I drank warm water, I kept getting the stink of sick, but I whistled as I walked.

And then I walked some more, and kept on going until the heat became unbearable and the ground shimmered as though ablaze. Grace was turned up to the max, swirling cool air around my scalp, but I was still overheating. There was no shade here, no way to cool off, so I stripped down and smothered myself in sunscreen then lay on my pack and draped my shirt loosely over my body and pulled Grace low over my eyes.

I lay there, baking in the midday sun, and prayed for something I knew seldom fell here. Rain.

It never came. There was nary a cloud, just blue, and the yellow of the desert. Nothing stirred, no breeze came to wash over me, no birds cried, no people passed, even the insects hid in their tiny tunnels where it was several degrees cooler.

Me, I lay prone, unmoving, and baked until I felt my head would explode.

The Cool of Night

My body spasmed, bringing me from sleep to wakefulness without that pleasant interlude where everything is fuzzy and the world is full of possibilities.

It was freezing. I shivered uncontrollably as I fumbled with numb hands to dress myself against the harshness of this barren wilderness. My teeth chattered as I tucked in my shirt then did up my jacket. The desert smelled strange at night, so different to England where every night, winter or summer, there was a dampness in the air. Here it was as empty and dry as space and the night stung my nostrils as I breathed in, overcome by a strange sense of being the only person left alive in a world that had finally decided enough was enough and eradicated humanity.

You could easily lose your mind at night, same as during the day, as the emptiness got to you, like standing on the moon and knowing you were a million miles away from your own kind, or I may as well have been for all the good it did me.

I had a short pee, my body holding on to what little moisture it could after my doze in the day, then I calmed my rumbling stomach with a few choice morsels of dried meats that had turned to something akin to old leather boots, and tasted even worse.

And then, like I'd done so often already, I walked.

Fed up with the whole damn thing, I decided I would not stop until I reached the village, where hopefully I could get the hell out of this place before the desert claimed me and slowly turned me to dust.

Not a Nice Heat

Acrid smoke stinging my nostrils brought me from my dream walk. My head snapped up and I sniffed several times—the unmistakable smell of burning rubber. Off in the distance I made out a pinprick of light, a torch in the emptiness. I knew different. It was a fire, and someone was burning something far from wholesome. No barbecue was this, but rather something vile and noxious.

It happened. We were far from anywhere, so many people disposed of their trash in the most obvious way. They burned it. Free heat, something to cook on if they were desperate, and it beat a big, stinky pile of trash.

At least it meant I'd made it. I was approaching the nameless village, and about time too. How long had I been gone? Already the days were confused and I dismissed it as unimportant. What difference did it make? It was a few days, certainly not a week, and I'd had a few adventures. It would be great to get a ride from the village to the main town, hop on a plane back to Dire Dawa, then go home.

Sure, I had a few things to sort out, like this damn artifact I'd been lumbered with, but I was confident I'd work something out, especially with the new and improved wards masking its, and thus my, location.

I sped up, keen to reach the sanctuary of the village, even though I knew I would find it quiet and deserted until the sun rose and people stirred from their slumber. Most got their work done during the first hours of daylight before the heat made doing anything but sitting somewhere shady a very bad idea.

The stink grew suddenly stronger, and I shook my head at the folly of setting fire to what I could only assume were old tires. I understood the logistics of getting shot of them, but surely they knew it was a bad idea? Different world, different ways, and I'd certainly done worse in my time.

The fire seemed strangely large though, but that was probably my tiredness and the desert playing games with scale.

Then I heard the screams.

Then the screams died.

Then there was silence. Which was worse.

I ran.

Blame the Old Guy

The village was nearly gone, what little there had been was razed to the ground. Adobe walls had collapsed under the intense heat as thatched roofs burned, steel buildings had buckled and fallen in on themselves, a few more robust buildings still stood, their contents destroyed, but solid construction was not the norm, so the place was eradicated.

Cars burned, blackened husks like oversized beetles, steaming with smoke, and everywhere was ash. The breeze blew it around the village like a macabre sandstorm, and I stood amid the carnage, smoke and ash swirling around me like I was walking through hell itself.

And the bodies, there were bodies everywhere. Most had died in their homes, several had been murdered as they made their escape, cut down by vicious wounds I knew were inflicted by magic. Most people were long dead, but several had just died, the ones I heard screaming, having been left for dead. What purpose did any of this serve? Why go to such despicable, cruel lengths to get my attention?

For I knew this was about me, or rather, what I carried.

"Curse you a million times over, Zewedu. This is all your fault," I screamed into the dawn. I felt like tearing at my flesh, pulling myself out of this corrupted carapace forever tainted by my involvement in this utter madness. Zewedu knew something like this would happen, that once the artifact was out in the world there would be those who would stop at nothing to get their hands on it, and he knew he would be putting my life and many of his countrymen's in danger. He didn't care, he wanted this thing taken far away from here, to be found, and had been more than willing to accept the consequences. Why? Because he knew he wouldn't be here to witness them.

Why couldn't it have remained where it was? Guess he'd thought it would be found sooner or later, that its power would seep out and somebody would retrieve it. But why did he care? Maybe he didn't. Maybe he wanted to test me, one final test of his pupil's strength, his might as a wizard after his tutelage. Or maybe it was merely because he was an insane old man and wanted a little fun even while he rotted forever in hell.

He'd got his wish. He'd brought that hell here, to his home.

The wind tore through the burning village, as angry as me at the massacre of innocents, and as the smoke buffeted up and away into the sky three ghostly silhouettes strode forward, angels of death bringing misery where once was happiness.

They picked the wrong fucking guy to mess with. I hadn't had any coffee for days, and wizards need coffee or they get grouchy.

"Game on, motherfuckers," I hissed as I ripped Wand from his slumber and shunted so much power through my system and into my hand that he physically caught fire.

I felt no pain. Only anger.

More Bad Guys

For such a vast country there sure seemed to be a lot of adepts in the vicinity. Maybe it was the emptiness that allowed even the slightest hint of powerful magic to be picked up on so easily, nothing else around to interrupt the flow, or maybe they'd spent a day or two traveling after sensing the artifact. Either way, they would soon join the others who'd tried to take what wasn't theirs and what they would use for undoubtedly nefarious means.

"You look too old for such work, brother," said a man with long, mousy hair and tanned skin, his Afrikaans accent strong, making him sound utterly foreign yet belonging at the same time.

"I'm not your brother, and you look fucking stupid in that jacket. What, you guys think you're cowboys or something?" Each wore a long, lightweight duster and a wide-brimmed hat that I had to admit looked nice. They were covered in the dust of the desert but it was overlaid with the ash of the fire, with the ash of the dead.

"Haha, just keeping cool and looking it too," said the man with a sneer.

"You did this?" I asked. "Why?"

"Get your attention, old man. Knew you'd be along soon enough to investigate. Who wouldn't?"

"So you murdered these people to get my attention?"

"No, they died so you'd know who you were dealing with. Hand it over, it will go better for you if you do. Give us the artifact and you can die quickly. Otherwise..." He left the threat hanging, as though I'd do as he asked. Man, these guys were jokers, even if callous ones.

"C'mon, you really think I'll give you anything?"

"I know you will, because if you don't me and my men will fuck you up so bad that—"

Why is it that people assume that after they threaten you, promise to do terrible things to get what they want, and then insult you, that you'll just stand there and have a chat, trade insults, until they deign it the time to carry out their threats? It never ceased to amaze me quite how stupid people could be.

Wand spat a fat chunk of a fireball at the blabbermouth even as I was already turning and blasting at the other two wizards who did their best to defend themselves. It must have been rather disconcerting, what with their leader screaming and batting at his head as his hat melted down what remained of his face. He fell to the floor, his legs kicked wildly, his arms thrashed, and then his head actually exploded.

"Good job, buddy," I said.

"Cheers, always wanted to do that," Wand replied happily.

I shook my head; Wand could be a worry at times.

The two men used their staffs to send shock waves of ferocious magic my way, but Wand was on form and volleyed like Darth Vader fighting good guys as he swished to and fro, batting the barbed magic right back at the men.

I dodged to the left and ducked behind a burned-out car as the smoke blew across the ground, blotting their view, and mine. Keeping low, I skirted around to the front of the ancient vehicle, dashed behind them silently, then charged at one man and launched myself into the air, landing with Wand embedded deep in the guy's skull. I yanked Wand free with magical assistance, a sick sucking noise like slurping thick milkshake through a straw totally grossing me out.

The other man turned and slammed his staff into my side, knocking me back. I stumbled on a rock and landed hard on my arse, backpack cushioning my fall somewhat, although the box jabbing into my back ruined that as a move I'd like to repeat.

He slammed down two-handed with the staff, sigils flaring, the end crackling with volatile magic, but I rolled aside and kicked him in the kneecap as I did so. No bone broke, but it hurt him just the same, and he collapsed as I scrambled to my feet. Our roles reversed, I booted aside his dropped staff and readied to deliver a death blow.

As Wand powered up and beautiful magic engorged my system, he did something unexpected. He began to cry. Not great wracking sobs, but gentle tears that streaked his cheeks and beaded in his unruly beard.

A stain spread at his crotch.

"You dare cry? You dare be afraid and piss your pants after what you did here?"

"I'm sorry, I'm sorry. Please don't kill me."

I killed him. Nothing worse than a whiner.

Energy spent, I slumped to the earth and sat there, despairing of just about everything in the world, but mostly the people who inhabited it.

I was beginning to hate Africa all over again.

The Dust Settles

After five minutes to catch my breath and wallow in self pity, I clambered awkwardly to my feet and shuffled about, unsure what to do, where to look, or if I should just close my eyes and wander about blindly. It couldn't be any worse than how things had been going already.

How to leave this place? How would I ever get home with so many people out to get me and what I had? Surely these guys had a vehicle? They must have, so where was it?

As if taking pity on me, the wind died down and the smoke cleared. I saw the true extent of the carnage wrought, which was no good thing, but at least I could investigate and find their vehicle. It didn't take long, and it didn't bode well. Their ineptitude had been complete, and the fools had managed to burn not only every other vehicle, including the one they'd stolen from me, but their own too. Guess they hadn't been expecting the wind, and it had blown the fires in all directions, leaving nothing but a burned out hire car that would have been nice and comfortable. It still had the sticker on the windscreen, a strange reminder of the modern world amid the battered vehicles dotted around the village.

Feeling the worst kind of nasty, I nonetheless scoured the village for anything of use, finding a big fat zero for my troubles, coming away with nothing but burned fingers and a soul-crushing sadness after witnessing so much needless, pointless death. In the end the stench of burned human flesh was what drove me back into the desert, that, and the need to punish myself maybe.

After all, this may have been Zewedu's doing, but I was to blame too. They were after me, after what I had, and I could have left it where I found it, let some other poor sap deal with the power the artifact contained. But I couldn't, could I? Because if these dark wizards got their hands on it it would be armageddon, and no, I'm not exaggerating.

To be purged of it all was my wish, but I had done too many bad things in my time to dare imagine my wish would become a reality. I would merely have to suffer and do what I always did. Grumble, but get on with it, and emerge victorious one way or another. Or if not victorious, then alive, which is always a good deal.

So I returned to the desert, knowing I had a long journey ahead of me, the longest journey of my life.

Seriously?

By day three of my travels after leaving the massacred village I was out of food, almost out of water, and sure as shit out of luck. Semi-delirious, smothered in sunscreen that was almost finished, and unable to walk another step, I sank to my knees in soft sand and looked to the sky for help, or inspiration, or maybe for a hungry bird to come peck out my eyes.

All I saw was blue. Flecks floated in my eyes, making it appear as though things were falling from the heavens. And then there came a sound from up above, as if these floaters had taken on form and were raining down on me. I knelt there, looking skyward, unmoving as a huge lump of mangled metal landed not three feet away. The impact sent sand billowing, and yet I remained motionless for I was unsure if this was real or a waking dream. It had to be a dream, lumps of metal didn't fall in the middle of the desert, did they?

When the dust settled, I stared at the deep crater and the globe of metal the size of a football that nestled in the ground like an oversized robot's egg.

"Just fucking great," I mumbled, before a tearing sound split the sky and it truly began to rain in the desert.

Not nice rain that you jump about in and stick out your tongue and taste that sweet, life-giving nectar, but a rain of death. Of metal and plastic and bodies and bits of things you have no name for.

The sky was ablaze now, as comets streaked then thudded to the ground all around me. Sand exploded high into the air as pieces of airplane shattered or buried deep and hissed.

With a sonic boom, a huge section of the rear of a small plane landed not far away; the tail fin stuck up like a beached whale.

Numb inside, I dodged the pieces of burning metal and walked to the large cylinder. Inside were several people still strapped to their seats, all were dead.

God forgive me, but I thanked my lucky stars as I took bottles of water from the pockets in the seats and snacks from their hands, and then I left, enough sustenance to keep me going for several more days.

Sometimes the desert is a funny place, but mostly not. All it holds is death, all it does is take, yet this day it gave back, and I wasn't sure if that was a good thing, or a very bad thing.

Things Get Dicey

I became lost to myself over subsequent days. No longer The Hat, no longer Arthur, no longer a wizard. No longer even a man.

What I became was nothing but heat, thirst, and hunger. A machine that continued, somehow, to put one foot in front of the other and slowly make its way back to civilization. There were no thoughts any longer, no memories good or bad, just pain and suffering that became so overwhelming it lost all meaning.

Had there ever been anything but this feeling? This all-encompassing discomfort that burrowed so deep into my flesh, my bones, my insides, that the lines blurred between pain and ecstasy? Hurt became so entrenched that it was a part of me now. My throat was raw and dry no matter that I still sipped occasionally on drops of warm water. My hunger was insatiable even though I chewed dried meat in tiny mouthfuls that left me constantly ravenous but stopped me dying.

My lips bled intermittently, blisters formed at the corners and pus congealed in my beard, the taste venomous. My skin burned and peeled until finally it must have grown dark and the incessant itching subsided, but my arms refused to tan properly and simply peeled to reveal raw, fresh flesh that burned all over again then repeated the cycle.

My boots held up well, but even so sand became a constant source of irritation. No matter how tight I tied the laces, or how often I tucked in my trousers, sand got everywhere. The rawness made every step an experiment in pain. Blisters popped, seeping milky, sometimes green liquid that crusted around my toes, sticking my socks to my feet. Every day when I stopped during the hottest hours and removed my boots I got deep knots of dread in my stomach before I tore my socks free, the skin along with them.

The smell was nauseating. My feet were rotting from my own bodily fluids, the stench of sweat combined with blood and pus so vomit-inducing that it made me purge.

Yet I thought little of it in the end, as this was what life was like in the desert and I was no longer a man, just this thing that walked and carried pain around with it like an old friend.

On and on it went, interminable suffering, until I was utterly empty inside. The worse it got, the more I walked, refusing to even stop during the worst of the day. Sometimes I found a few sticks and lit a fire at night and huddled beside it, dropping off into sleep consumed by nightmares. More often I simply fell, exhausted, and slept until I awoke then clambered to my feet and continued my journey.

Was there a point to this? Where was I going, and why? I refused to think about such things, merely walked, not hoping to reach my destination, not wishing to remain in the desert.

Just walking.

Days blurred until they had no meaning. I grew thin and wiry, stringy like a desert rabbit, until my trousers were loose and I reached the last notch on my belt.

For some reason I still carried a small spade. It was a constant annoyance yet I refused to leave it behind, something telling me I would need it one day, if only to dig myself a shallow grave I could climb into and finally be at peace, at rest.

And on it went, day after interminable day, a creature of the desert now, truly at home. This was where I belonged, where I was meant to be. To suffer, to be purged, to be beaten down and forced to become nothingness.

Mind empty, body failing, covered in blisters and burns and carrying the most important artifact in history upon my back, I was the chosen one, being tested in the desert to see if I was worthy of such a prize. I became utterly mad, had visions of God-like status, that I was special, singled out for this quest as no other could accomplish it, and yet I knew I was a fool, that I was merely a man, nothing special, but even then I refused to truly believe it. Surely I was the chosen one, being tested beyond human endurance to emerge as something all-powerful, to be worshiped and adored?

Nope, just a twat in a hat wandering around where he should know better.

I cackled at the thought; at least I hadn't lost it completely. I still remembered I was me, the memory was in there somewhere, and when I got too nutty thoughts surfaced enough to remind me I was nothing but a fool. Not exactly a great consolation, but at least it stopped me doing anything stupid like seeing if I could sprout wings like an angel and fly out of there.

I couldn't, could I?

Lying face down in the sand, I shook my head. No, I couldn't fly, but it was worth a try.

"What are you doing?" asked a voice as a shadow loomed over me.

"Seeing if I can fly like an angel," I somehow managed to reply.

"Can you?" asked the voice, genuinely intrigued.

"I'm not sure, don't think so. Am I on a cloud?"

There was a long pause. "No, but you are on my lawn."

I turned my head and lifted it slightly. I was staring at grass. Beautiful, green, lush grass.

I licked it. Then I passed out.

A Mirage

I awoke, as I so often did, to plenty of strangeness. For one, I felt damp. Not in a shivery, this is crap kind of way, but in a lovely, comforting, feels like home kind of way. I was on my back, and as I clenched my fists I grabbed handfuls of what felt like grass. Delicious, damp grass.

I could hear humming nearby, someone happily pottering about, immersed in their task.

Had I really lost consciousness on somebody's lawn out in the middle of the desert? Haha, no of course I hadn't. I was delirious, or dreaming, or had finally lost the plot and gone utterly gaga. With a shrug, figuring I had nothing to lose, I opened my eyes and risked becoming severely disappointed.

"What the...?" I croaked, before falling into an extended coughing fit that hurt so much I was surprised my larynx didn't jump out of my mouth and crawl screaming under the nearest rock.

"Ah, you're awake," came a jolly voice, his shadow so welcome. Shade was something alien now, all there had been was sun and then the emptiness of the night. "Thought it best to leave you where you lay. Never know what damage you can do to a fellow when he's in your condition. Feeling better?" he asked brightly, his clipped British accent so at odds with everything I half-expected him to offer me a nice—

"Cup of tea?" he asked, finishing my thought, before he turned and walked away, whistling as he went.

Somehow, and to this day I don't know how I managed it, I got to my feet. My eyes were blurry, vision was so poor I dared not move, so I stood there, swaying, until the dizziness passed and the crustiness around my raw eyes melted down my cheeks because of my tears. I was amazed I had enough liquid to spare, but what can I tell you, it was an emotional time.

And then I cried all over again. Tears of joy, of disbelief, of confusion, and yes, of concern for my mental wellbeing, because this could not be happening, was impossible, so I lamented the loss of all I had been, all I was, knowing I'd been beaten by the desert this time.

"Come on, old chap, tea's getting cold," came the polite shout of a man I was yet to see more than in silhouette.

I rubbed at my sore eyes and focused properly on where the sound was coming from. Across a large, perfectly manicured lawn, a head stuck out the side of a smart but rustic open veranda made from thick branches and mud infill under a thatched roof. It felt colonial somehow, grand yet basic, comfortable and inviting, cool and airy. And there was shade! Proper, full shade, and benches and chairs and a table and a silver tray with a teapot and two cups and saucers. There were even biscuits! Biscuits! I drooled as I stumbled across the lawn in an utter daze and nodded dumbly at the man who skipped across the expansive decking then took a seat in a wicker chair. He nodded a head of shocking white hair combed back like a World War 2 picture card soldier and as I eased into the chair opposite he beamed up at me then said, "One lump or two?"

"Huh?"

"Sugar, dear boy, one lump or two? Milk? Oh, what am I saying? Of course you have milk. All respectable English gentleman have milk. I'll give you two lumps, you look like you could do with it." He poured the tea with steady, gnarled hands, used a pair of tiny tongs to add two lumps of sugar to both cups, then poured the milk before stirring gently.

The tinkling of a silver teaspoon against bone china was truly bizarre.

"Drink, drink, quench that thirst. My, you are in a bad way, aren't you? Get lost did you? Been for a wander and took a wrong turn? Run out of petrol? I always tell people, stock up, carry more of everything than you think you could possibly need, it's the only way to survive."

"No, it wasn't like that," I mumbled, then reached for my tea. My hand shook so much that I had to use two to hold the cup, but the sugary aroma was divine and no way did I want to spill a drop. It would be sacrilegious under such circumstances.

The warm, strong, sugar-laden liquid hit my tastebuds in an almost orgasmic explosion that sent my head reeling. My body surged with the energy boost until I thought I'd faint. I drank greedily yet carefully, my parched lips stung, my throat protested at such a deluge of water, and my stomach had no idea what to do with all this goodness. Sugar coursed through my veins, I became lightheaded, and as I set the cup back down gently on the saucer I truly believed I might even survive this battle with Mother Desert.

"Another?" he asked, smiling at me.

"Please."

He uncrossed his legs, his white linen trousers creased down the front sharper than my razor, then poured me another cup of tea.

I took it slower this time, but still had no words, just drank and enjoyed the feeling of life being restored to my battered body. I could focus on nothing but the man and the tea, and for now that was enough. I got the feeling there would be time enough to investigate my surroundings, try to make sense of it all, so for now I sat and drank and smiled stupidly at this old man, like a blast from the colonial past, as he watched me intently, nothing but friendly curiosity on his lined, deeply tanned face.

"Biscuit?"

I nodded.

"Take two, dear boy, you need it."

I took two.

A New Friend

We sat in comfortable silence for some time. How long that might have been I couldn't possibly say. Time meant nothing to me, I was too far gone. The tea, the biscuits, and plenty of water, slowly brought me back to myself, and that in itself was a mistake. I came to understand that I was not very well, that everything hurt in ways I hadn't thought possible, or had done my utmost to forget.

My head throbbed, my limbs were burned and covered in sores, my face felt like it was being chewed on by ants, and my feet, oh my poor feet. I actually had to check they were there. It felt like they had been chopped off and the stumps were being jabbed at with sharp sticks by someone inordinately angry with me. They were still there, more's the pity.

The water eased the rawness of my throat and eventually I felt I could talk a little, albeit slowly and rather hoarsely.

"Thank you, I appreciate the help," I managed to say before having to take a few rough swallows which led to several minutes of painful coughing.

"My pleasure. Now, why don't you tell me how it is you're in my garden?" He leaned his wiry frame forward; his clean-shaven chin twitched as he waited expectantly. A gentle warm breeze ruffled his pale blue shirt.

"I'm trying to get to the next town, can't remember its name, so I can get a flight back to the city, then home."

"Ah, yes, you're going the right way, although you do have rather a long way to go yet."

"How far?"

"About fifty or so miles. Where have you come from?"

I described the village that had been razed, not wanting to get into the whole dead master thing, and all that.

"That's quite the journey you've made already," he said with a whistle. "All through the desert on foot?"

"Yeah," I grumbled, staring down at my poor battered feet.

"You wait right there, I have just the answer." My host hopped to his feet and was gone.

I sighed and leaned back in the chair, unable to quite reconcile myself with what was happening. How was this real? How was he here out in the middle of the desert with a damn lawn and a colorful array of flowers and shrubs, this large house, the veranda, any of it?

I got up, every movement painful, and walked to the edge of the veranda where I leaned against the railing and stared out at the garden. The lawn wrapped around the property by the looks of it, with small areas of dense planting, irrigation carefully hidden behind the plants. A large sprinkler system suddenly came to life, drenching the lawn. At the edge of the property huge boulders marked the boundary, and fertile soil slowly gave way to the desert where the moisture leached away and everything returned to barren wilderness once more.

It made absolutely no sense.

We were smack bang in the middle of nowhere, so how, and why, was he living here?

My thoughts were interrupted by the clattering behind me.

"Come, sit down," my host offered as he poured boiling water from a kettle into a large, well-worn metal bowl.

I returned to my seat and sat, thinking I was to freshen up.

"If I may?" he asked, nodding to my feet.

"May what?" I asked, confused.

"Your feet, my dear boy. They stink to high heaven and they must surely be sore. I will clean them for you."

"No, I can't let you do that. I'll do it, but thank you for the kind offer. I'm Arthur by the way."

"I insist. You are my guest, and I will clean your feet."

Without further ado, and despite my continued protestations, he carefully removed my boots then peeled off my socks, what was left of them, which wasn't much.

My feet were worse than I'd imagined, and how he could stand the sight of them, let alone the smell, was a miracle. They were utterly disgusting and terribly damaged.

He carefully wiped them clean of the worst of the blood and pus with a soft cloth then bathed my feet in the warm bowl, him on his knees prone before me. It felt so wrong, so strange, and the kindness of the gesture brought me to tears once more. He smiled up at me, telling me everything would be all right, that he would look after me. I had never known such kindness, certainly not from a stranger, and it gave me hope, gave me strength, and damn but it felt nice.

This man had a soft, gentle touch, as though he were a nurse, but I knew that wasn't the case, that he had his own tale to tell. This was no ordinary man stuck out here. He must have done things, seen things, lived a life worthy of tales that should be told, but now wasn't the time, or the place, and I realized he hadn't even told me his name.

After he finished cleaning my feet best he could, certainly better than I possibly could have, he applied a thick green poultice then wrapped them in bandages.

"It will take a while to heal, several days until you can even walk properly, and you will need new socks."

"Thank you so much, I don't know what to say."

"Don't mention it. If you can't help a stranger in need then who can you help? Now, I assume you would like some dinner? I insist you stay until you are healed. I have a spare room, a clean bed with fresh sheets, and you are welcome to remain until you are ready to continue."

"That sounds perfect. Are you alone out here?"

"There will be plenty of time for questions later. For now, let me go make dinner and we can talk then. Sit, relax, enjoy the shade. I shall return." He gathered up the bowl and cloths then left me to the silence.

Weird and Wonderful

I watched the sun set from the cool of the veranda, a true luxury. Damn but it was beautiful out here. Beautiful but so very, very strange. Already the trek across the desert had become nothing but a dream, my recollection of it akin to a dimly recalled movie where I could picture myself stumbling about, staggering over dunes, gasping for breath like a fish out of water, watching my skin burn and crackle.

Of course, there were no such images to recall, it was merely how I pictured it. What was real, and disconcerting, was the state I was in. Now I had been given sustenance, and the adrenaline had receded, I had a clear enough head to take note of what my body had been telling me for days. Basically, I was screwed. Everything hurt, everything was either crusty, peeling, or cracking and oozing. Ugh, such ooze.

I had no strength, I had no muscle mass as I'd been eating away at myself just to stay alive, and I had no possibility of continuing my journey for many days. If I hadn't reached this place, I knew with utter certainty

I would be dead by the morning, or so close to it I would be unable to move.

This stranger had saved me, he had shown unparalleled kindness, and it freaked me out.

What was his name? How had he set this up here? And why on earth would he want to?

Guess I'd find out soon enough. Main thing was, I could relax. He was a nice guy, had assisted me in my hour of need, and he made a mean cup of tea even though normally I wouldn't go near the stuff. Wizards drink coffee, and lots of it, but beggars can't be choosers, and I was a sorry looking beggar so would take what was offered with the utmost gratitude.

The desert cooled and the animals emerged from their hiding places. Barks and strange calls rang out across the plains. Some would hunt, others would be hunted. Some would survive and flourish, others would perish. Such is the way of the world, as things should be, but for once, for this night, I was exempt from the fight for survival. I had already been saved.

Delightful aromas wafted my way and set my mouth to watering. While we waited for dinner, I took the opportunity to explore the setup here before darkness made it impossible. I needn't have worried, as before I stepped off the veranda lights came on everywhere. The garden was lit beautifully, the rustic house too.

The veranda faced west and ran the whole length of one wall. The rest of the property was basic but large, a huge wood-framed building made using whole tree trunks with smaller branches criss-crossing this way and that all under a thick thatched roof. It was akin to the communal village gathering halls, but with more attention to detail and a damn sight larger, but it was typical of the region and wouldn't look out of place anywhere local.

There were hints of this being a far from regular build, subtle details that told of fine craftsmanship and time taken selecting just the right piece of wood for its location, and there was glass at the windows, uncommon outside of the towns and cities.

The roof also housed a large array of solar panels, enough to run such a large home with all modern conveniences. I got the impression my host didn't slum it.

It was impressive, but disconcerting, as a lot of trouble had been taken building this place, and it wasn't like it would be easy to get the materials out here. Did he have a vehicle? Surely he must have? Could I get a lift? I bloody hoped so.

"Ah, there you are," said the man with a huge smile. "Having a look around, eh?"

"If that's okay?"

"Of course. Do you want a tour of the inside? Dinner will be ten minutes or so. I hope you're hungry?"

My stomach rumbled in answer and we both laughed. "You can take that as a definite yes."

"Come," said the man as he turned to a low front door, "I will show you how I live in this desert."

I ducked through the doorway and he closed it behind me. I jumped at the sound but he just smiled.

"Don't want to let the bugs in. Little buggers they are."

I turned to face the room.

Nice Pad

We were in a living room, and it was both how I'd expected and not. It was simply furnished with rugs over a concrete floor, several oversized sofas, and a large wingback chair with a small antique table holding a reading light and several books.

Local carvings and blankets hung on the walls, while much of the furniture was antique and very British. This was a house from a different time, a style no longer in fashion, but it was remarkably clean, very organized, and very comfortable to be in.

"You've put a lot of work in here," I commented.

"All done by my own two hands," he said, smiling sheepishly.

"Wow, impressive."

"Let me show you the rest."

I took the tour, going from the living room to a large kitchen with modern appliances and a huge rough plank table, not a match on my kitchen of course, but certainly better than anything you'd find for several hundred miles.

There were several bedrooms, a tiled bathroom as well as en-suites, and then we were back out to the veranda. This was obviously where he spent most of his time.

"Sit, let's have a drink before dinner."

We both sat and he poured us two iced teas from a large jug full of lemon slices and ice cubes. It seemed odd to have a cold drink now yet a hot one earlier, but we all have our peccadilloes and frankly I was just happy to drink anything wet.

"Ah, so nice to have company out here. It's been a while."

"Guess you don't get many people passing by," I said, sipping my drink and loving it.

"No, not many. Sometimes it's years between guests. I do hope you will stay awhile."

"I will, if that's all right. A few days, just to get better. Unless..." I ventured.

"Ah, I'm sorry, and I knew you'd ask, but I'm afraid I don't have a vehicle any longer."

"Oh." I couldn't hide my disappointment.

"A fellow comes once a month to stock me up with everything I need, takes me to town if I want, but I don't drive these days."

"May I ask why? Seems like you'd want to out here, just in case you run out of anything."

"The desert gives me everything I require," he said with a knowing wink.

"Ah, right."

"I don't drive because I don't want the distraction of a vehicle. If I have a car I will be going back and forth, leaving this place, getting embroiled in the nonsense of the towns, venturing further afield, and what would that achieve? Nothing. I am where I want to be, and I want to focus on the now, be truly here, not tempted by the outside world."

"Makes sense. Sorry for asking, it's just, you know."

"I understand entirely, my dear fellow, think nothing of it. Now, shall we eat?"

My stomach rumbled again and we both laughed.

"I'll take that as another yes," he said as he got up to leave

A Lovely Dinner

Dinner was divine. Admittedly, anything but sweaty dried meat would have tasted amazing, but even in my messed-up state I could appreciate just how great a cook my host was. I was expecting a formal setting at the dining table, but it seemed he'd embraced many local ways so we ate informally out on the veranda, using our fingers to pick at many and varied bowls and plates. From dates to dried apricots, slivers of meat to fluffy cous cous, nuts, and a local bread I'd always loved, we licked our fingers and washed it down with glasses of milk.

We spoke about the desert, about its beauty and hostility, about how it brings out the truth of a person and how dangerous a place it could be. He told me tales of the building, how it took him several years and quite a lot of trouble to finish the construction. How hard it was to get his furniture out here that had been in storage for many years, and the difficulty he had in convincing locals to sell him the materials he needed and for him to learn the skills necessary to build such a home.

But it was all vague, he didn't actually tell me anything about how long he'd lived here, what he did before, what his previous life had been like, his family, his vocation, or even his bloody name.

It got to a point that I didn't want to ask, fearing he'd already told me and I'd been too far gone to remember.

Something was up with this guy, as nobody in their right mind lived like this, so alone, unless they were running from something. But that was his business. Everyone had their own demons to fight. I didn't intrude, didn't pry, just let him say what he wanted, take it as far as he wished, and as the night wore on I sensed he was finally relaxing in my company, confident I wouldn't pry in affairs that were none of my business.

I told him of my family, some of my life, but kept the whole wizard thing quiet, as it would only lead to complications. So we were like two peas in a pod, talking yet not really talking. Not telling lies yet not telling the whole truth either. But surely that's just how humans interact, isn't it? There is always more to tell, but some things are private. We enjoyed each other's company and had a nice evening, and I got the impression he was just as grateful as me for the companionship, the chance to talk to another human being.

Eventually I must have nodded off as I awoke to him gently shaking my shoulder. He smiled at me; time for bed.

He showed me to my room then pulled the door closed.

I lay down on the soft mattress and was asleep immediately.

When I woke up the sun was shining, didn't it always, and the day was already warm. But in a nice way. The room faced away from the rising sun and had only a tiny window offering a view out over the desert; I could have happily stayed there for days.

Carefully, I got off the bed and muttered to myself about being a terrible guest when I saw the mess I'd made of the sheets. I should have showered, or at least undressed, but going to bed without my dirty clothes on would probably have made even more of a mess.

I pulled off the sheets and bundled them up then headed into the small en-suite. I stripped, had the best pee of my life, then turned on the shower. The water was cool and refreshing and I stood there, unmoving, for minutes while the desert sluiced away. Then I carefully washed myself down, mindful not to rub too hard at the many and surprisingly varied wounds I had, until I was as clean as I could get. Then I removed the bandages from my feet and soaked them for a while until I felt like a new, if still somewhat battered man.

It all got rather depressing when I looked in the mirror though. I hardly recognized myself. My beard was wild, my hair the same, and my face was red and blistered. Patches of skin were pink and raw, my eyes were crusty, my lips bled, and the rest of my body wasn't much better. I was tanned dark on neck and arms but much of it was peeling already, and I knew I was in for a terrible few days as the skin sloughed off. The new growth would be sensitive and much of it would scab over. Still, at least I had the opportunity to recover. Better that than the alternative.

At the thought, my stomach flipped over. This wasn't done yet. I still had, what, fifty or so miles to go? Ah well, I could do that. A few nights of walking if I was sensible about things, and then it would be plain sailing after that.

I took a white dressing gown from the back of the door and gathered up my clothes with the bedding then went out into the kitchen to ask if I could use the washing machine, assuming there was one. And that was another question I'd forgotten to ask. Where did he get his water?

"Morning, Arthur," said the strange man. "Sleep well?" he asked with a knowing smile.

"Morning. And I slept like a baby. What time is it?"

"Oh, still early. About six-thirty."

"Man, I feel like I slept longer than that."

"Oh, you did, dear boy. You slept all through the day and night yesterday, so it's no wonder you rose early this morning."

"Wow," I said, scratching my beard, "guess I needed it. Um, sorry, I got the bedding dirty, do you have a machine?"

"Yes, over there." He pointed to a washing machine in the corner. "But don't trouble yourself. You are my guest, I will clean all your clothes and have them smelling delightful and as soft as your bed. You relax."

"You sure? It feels strange you doing so much for me, not that I'm ungrateful."

"Of course. It's nice to have someone to look after. I miss it." He stared off into the distance. I didn't pry.

"Then thank you, you are very kind."

He took my laundry and as he loaded up the machine said, "Be a good fellow and make coffee."

"Sure, I could do with a few cups."

So I made coffee. Utter heaven.

We sat outside and enjoyed the shade while the sun rose, sipping coffee and talking about this and that. It already felt like we were old friends, The Hat and this mystery man of the desert.

Things were looking up.

A Bit Awkward

"Here, let me," said the man after we'd enjoyed a breakfast of eggs and meat and were back in the kitchen. "I'll do the rest of your washing." He moved to take my backpack from the chair where I'd left it, but I hurried over and took it from him.

"Sorry, it's just, um, I'm a bit funny about my stuff, might be something sharp in there. Don't want you getting hurt."

"Absolutely, I didn't mean to pry. I wasn't being nosy."

"Of course not, but who knows what I have in there after the trip I've had? Look, there's even a spade. Don't know why I carried it all this way. Might be snakes or daggers in there too," I said, trying to claw back my rudeness.

"I'm sure it's fine, but if you have anything to be washed then just leave it by the machine." He wandered off and I felt awful for my behavior but the last thing I wanted was him asking questions about the box. I shouldn't have been so lax, leaving it like this. Shows the state I was in. Hell, I shouldn't even be here. What if someone tracked me down and brought trouble to his door? I should go.

I checked the wards and they were still intact. Nobody could track me to this location, only the general area, and very general at that. But that didn't mean they wouldn't come. It wasn't as if there was much else of interest in the area.

Another day, and then I would have to leave. I wouldn't be able to live with myself if I caused problems for this odd, somehow mesmerizing man.

I took out the rest of my clothes and set them in the basket by the washing machine then took the bag to my room and left it beside the bed. He wouldn't pry, he was too much of a gentleman.

My raggedy clothes were dry almost as soon as he hung them out so I dressed and although still looking a mess I was at least a clean mess. To repay his kindness I helped with the chores, watering the garden, cleaning the kitchen, my specialty, and sweeping off the veranda. Then we broke for a light lunch which ended up being not so light as I was ravenous after skipping a day, and as the afternoon wore on we did less and less until the heat became too much and we retired indoors.

He usually read at this time, so I left him to his comfy chair and his books and went for a lie down. It goes to show how out of whack I was as I fell asleep almost immediately and didn't wake up until dusk.

Feeling better for the sleep, and amazed I could actually rest this much, I trimmed my beard down to stubble and even managed to get a comb through my hair. Now I looked more like me, not something dragged from under a rock. Still unkempt and wild, but manageable.

We followed the same routine as the first night. He cooked, we ate, and we chatted as we tucked in to a fine repast. As the night came, the true night, we settled down with cups of tea and talked.

What a Life

I don't know what it was about the old man, but I was very relaxed in his company. What should have been weird was quite the opposite. He was one of those people who are easy to talk to, who you feel like you've known for years after only a few hours in their company. He was guarded, same as me, but in that friendly way where you both understand that everyone has a past and maybe they don't want to share all of it with you or anyone else.

As the night settled and we did the same, warmed by drinks and each other's company, we relaxed in his living room and got comfortable on the plush chairs. How odd this all was, chilling out in chairs that wouldn't be out of place in the UK but certainly were here in the desert. Surrounded by reminders of home, yet definitely African at the same time, it made my head spin if I thought about it. So I didn't. I enjoyed my host's company and felt more at ease than since I stepped foot on this cursed continent.

He told me a little of his past, of a wife and a life far from here, of work and weekends traveling the country with the love of his life, both keen walkers, explorers. But there had always been a wanderlust and he had traveled extensively in his youth, so the weekend hikes wouldn't cut it. They ventured further afield, and more regularly, until he found that wasn't enough either. Eventually, he'd packed up work, sold his business, and he and his wife began traveling in earnest.

You name it, he'd been there. He told me of many places, of adventures that made me laugh then gasp as he spun his tales of danger and excitement. For years they roamed, always seeking new things, always looking for the next remote place to visit, the next series of interesting characters to encounter.

But it was never enough, and they, or rather, he, couldn't stop. No sooner had they arrived somewhere than he was thinking of the next trip, the next location. Visits back home grew increasingly infrequent, until his wife had put her foot down and told him she'd had enough, that she couldn't keep up the pace. They were getting older and should slow down, rest up a while, maybe even stop their roaming.

He'd promised he would, that whatever it was he was searching for wasn't to be found anywhere else, that he had what he wanted in her, the love of his life, and that was enough for him.

It was all a lie of course, he'd been fooling himself. Life back home felt mundane and boring, and he felt trapped. Soon he began traveling alone, looking for something but he didn't know what, spending less and less time at home.

Once, when he returned, he asked her one more time if she would come away with him, a final trip before he gave it all up, and she agreed. They came here, and she loved it. The peace, the open space, the solitude, and the people. This was what she had been searching for, she had said, this felt like home, true home. He agreed. This was where he was meant to be, where they were both meant to be. To grow old together, without distraction, to be one with the desert and the sky, part of the land, part of the history of this ageless place.

They returned home to make arrangements, to sell their house and cut what few ties they had with a life that already felt like someone else's.

Disaster struck. She became ill, and grew worse at an alarming rate. He cared for her at home, plans of relocation forgotten, but within six months she was dead and he was alone.

For several years he remained in the old home, unable to do much of anything, lost without her even though he'd spent much of the last few years traveling alone. But she had always been there waiting for him, and it had always given him comfort, given him the drive he needed to continue his travels, determined to see all there was to see of the world. Now she was gone and he gave up.

One day, after watching a TV show of all things, he made a decision. He would make the move, carve out a life for himself in this inhospitable place. Not for her, but for him. Of course, in truth it was for her memory, to show her he could stick to their plan and finally settle and if not be happy then at least be at peace with the past and maybe make a future for himself.

So he sold up, moved out here, bought some land, and began to build. It took years, and it was not without its troubles along the way, but he'd made it. He'd done what they had decided to do, and he was happy here.

It was some story, and there were clearly things missing from the tale, but it rang true. A wanderer who'd finally found a home. It sounded so familiar because he was like me. This was why we were so relaxed in each other's company. We'd both been searching for something and had found it. I had searched for many years for an answer to the biggest question of all. What's the point? And I had found it first with magic but even that hadn't been enough to satisfy me and I knew there was still much missing.

No, I'd finally found it with George and Penelope. When I looked into Penelope's eyes and made her drop her shopping on the high street I knew there and then that she was what I'd been searching for my whole life.

We were the same, lost souls looking for an answer to this thing called life, and we may have discovered it in very different places but the result was the same. The knowledge that this was right, this was good, this was how things were meant to be.

"And on that note, I will bid you goodnight," said my host, smiling at me after I'd told him how alike we were.

"Goodnight."

He nodded and left.

I stayed up late that night, lost in thought, wondering if I'd ever make it home to the family that gave my life meaning.

Bloody Typical

"Sorry, old chap, but I knew it would turn up eventually. Good job I checked your bag, eh? I have waited so long for this, dreamed of it every night for years, searched the world for it, and yet I was unable to uncover its location. But I knew, I just knew, that if I waited patiently it would find me. And now it has." My host smiled sadly at me then looked at the box with pure excitement.

His hands shook, in fact his whole body was trembling with anticipation. He was crying, fine tears that ran along the creases of his weathered face then dripped silently to the floor.

"So it was all a lie?" I asked, sitting up in bed and staring at him over by the doorway.

"What we spoke of last night? No, not a lie. I did those things, I lived that life, and I never told my wife what I was searching for. She never knew who I really was, what I was. A wizard like you. A magic user, an adept, and I regret it to this day. All of it was true," he said wistfully, lost to the memories. "We traveled, I searched, and just by luck we chose this place for our final trip. Oh, how can I describe the feeling to you when we came here? I knew this was it, that this was where the artifact was hiding. I knew it was a matter of time, nothing more. Her death almost made me give up. I felt so useless, like a fool, but then I understood this was my fate, my destiny. I waited so long, and I was right to wait. You brought it to me, now my search is over."

"You helped me. Did you know then, is that why you were so kind?"

"What? No, of course not, dear boy. I always help the lost, the injured, those in need. I'm not a monster, just an old man waiting to fulfill his destiny."

"And that destiny involves locking those in need inside what is clearly a very well thought out prison?" I asked, taking in the room within a room I found myself in.

"I'm not an imbecile," he snapped, locking eyes with me after reluctantly looking away from the box and what it contained.

"Could have fooled me. What, watched Silence of the Lambs before you locked yourself away out here?"

"It's not the walls that make the prison, although they certainly help," he mused. "It's the level of magic involved. I am an old practitioner, Arthur, way beyond your level, and the wards embedded in this glass go beyond anything you are capable of, have probably ever experienced in your life. I was there when the glass was made, I put my very being into these panels as they were produced, and then I spent many a day and night harnessing this wondrous universal power to ensure the wards could never be broken."

"Blah, blah, blah. Whatever." I may have sounded casual, even bored, but inside I was freaked out and very concerned. I sat up properly in bed and fluffed up my pillows as though his blathering was of little concern to me, but I knew for a fact he was right.

I was trapped, I was next to useless, and I was at his mercy. Plus, he had the artifact. Which meant I was well and truly screwed.

Time to Reflect

"You have what you need. I will return soon." The old wizard clutched the box tight then turned and left.

The bedroom was halved in size now, surrounded on all sides by thick glass that shimmered if you looked at it just right. He'd left a portable chemical toilet inside the prison, along with a jug of water, bowls, flannels, soap, even my toothbrush and some toothpaste. There was also dried fruit and meat plus bottles of water. What a very thoughtful jailer.

He'd gone to some serious lengths, not to mention incredible forward-planning, to have constructed this. Guess that explained the strange gaps in the wooden cladding I'd thought were a quirky design feature but which allowed this cage to unfold when he had his prey cornered. No wonder he'd built the place himself. Why go to this trouble? Because he didn't know who would turn up, what they would be like or what he'd have to do to claim the artifact as his own.

My guess was the whole place was rigged in a similar style. Multiple traps laid out to capture whoever came in a variety of ways depending on whether they were friend or foe. Well, I'd been a friend and look where that had got me. Locked in a bloody glass cage like Hannibal Lecter. Bastard. And I'd liked the old guy too, felt like we were one and the same, his life almost a mirror of my own in so many ways. Both of us searching for something. But he'd been one of the nutjobs who spent their whole life running around the world looking for artifacts rather then getting on with their lives.

There were loads of people like him, both wizards and the merely curious. Those who'd heard stories of magic or magical items and went to extremes to find such artifacts. Some even succeeded.

Things, stuff, whatever that might be, are never the answer to that nagging feeling you get in your stomach when you lie awake at night wondering what's missing from your life. It's never about the stuff, it's always about you, about how you have lived your life, about how you are living your life. It's about doing what's right, about finding your place in this world. A purpose, a family, a home, somewhere to feel safe, to be grateful for what you have, not always searching for something else, because you'll never find it unless you give yourself the opportunity to be happy. They never learned though, they kept on looking and when they found what they wanted, this mythical artifact or magic in my case, they soon realize it isn't the whole truth, the answer to why they have this empty feeling inside, it just exacerbates the problem.

And here I was, stuck with a man who'd built a house-sized trap in the Ethiopian desert in the hope that one day the artifact would come his way.

Guess he'd got what he wanted.

Almost.

I smiled as, right on cue, he stormed through the door and scowled at me.

"You aren't the only one who knows a thing or two about wards, old boy," I emphasized, giving him my most winningest of smiles.

"I will have it," he whispered, despair filling his eyes. "I have waited too long to be denied it now. Don't make me do anything I will regret, Arthur. I will give you time to think about it as I am, after all, a patient man, but do not try my patience too far. It will behove you to lift the wards and let me have what is mine by right."

"By right?" I asked, incredulous. "What right do you have to it?"

"It is my destiny. I found this place, I searched the globe and yet I found this place when I'd given up hope, stopped my search. It's destiny. It is mine." He left.

I was absolutely dying for a pee so I went and had one. It wasn't far.

Stockholm Syndrome

For seven days and seven nights I peed in a glorified bucket, pooed in the same receptacle, washed myself as best I could, brushed my teeth twice a day, and even got to grips with some stubborn knots in my hair. I combed my beard, trimmed my toenails, topped up magic in the Quiet Place every single morning until I was brimming with the good stuff, and yet I mostly lay on the bed, not sleeping, just recovering.

By the end of my week of incarceration I awoke to find myself healed. The daily magic dose had worked wonders, allowing me to speed up recuperation until finally I became The Hat again. No sore feet, no aches or pains apart from the usual dodgy knees, and even my blistered skin had shed, the new skin had lost its rawness, and I was truly back to my old self.

I was well fed, had a simple breakfast and lunch every day but my host was generous with the evening meal and supplied sumptuous feasts. Maybe he was trying to win me over, maybe he was a good guy deep down, or maybe it was a habit born out of daily ritual for years on end that ensured he shared his culinary skills with me daily.

He was also utterly stark raving mad by now. Every day he would come and deliver my food and every day he would ask me the same damn thing.

Had I changed my mind? Would I lift the wards so he could access the artifact? At least just enough so he could see it, maybe touch it?

And every day my answer had been the same. No, no, and no.

He grew increasingly frantic, his manner more erratic by the day, until I feared for his safety. I was secure inside my jail, he was loose out there doing who knew what. I heard his shouts and moans of frustration as I sensed a disturbance in the magical force, felt him pushing things to the limits, calling upon untold spells both benign and perilous, using magic that was out-of-bounds to most, too frightening for any but the most adept.

He tried everything to break my wards, used spells I'd heard of but never mastered to break the bonds of my will, but they all failed. One thing I was very good at was protection. Not perfect, but pretty damn good, and I knew he wouldn't break them. They were too much a part of me, imbued with my essence, and even if I died they would remain.

One thing I knew for certain, and him too, hence his increasing frustration, was that he'd never get into that box.

I think I was more bored than I'd ever been in my entire life. More bored than when I went on honeymoon and had to endure two weeks of sand up my bottom. At least then there had been lots of sex and wine, here there was just the room, and even the sand wasn't allowed access. Which was a bonus.

But at least it would have been a distraction. I was bored, bored, bored.

Oh, and he was becoming increasingly homicidal.

Gone was the nice guy. In its place was this somewhat demented, whiny, shouty, pleading, sometimes begging, sorry excuse for a man who sulked because he couldn't have what he wanted. He was a slim fellow to start with, but in the space of a week he'd become emaciated. He eyes were sunken and dark underneath, his skin was sallow, he'd lost his tan, veins stood proud on his arms, nothing but skin and bone, and his cheeks were so sharp they were ready to burst through the skin. His hair had lost its sheen, the luster replaced with a dank oily coating, and he wasn't brushing it. He smelled bad too. And yet he continued to cook, to sometimes be polite, to other times rant and rave, and his frustration grew by the day.

It was understandable. He'd got so close only to be denied at the last hurdle. Tough, he wasn't about to get his twisted hands on this. I had no idea what he wanted to do with it, he was yet to tell me, so maybe I should ask? Maybe I was the one being silly and he should have it? After all, he didn't seem like a bad guy, in fact I kinda like him. Who was I to judge? Who was I to decide? Maybe he had every right to it. Maybe it really was his destiny to own the artifact, safeguard it, protect it? Why not him instead of me? I certainly didn't want it anyway.

Yeah, I'd ask him why he'd searched for it his whole adult life. Hell, I assumed he'd become a wizard in order to find it, or maybe once he learned of magic he learned of the artifact? Either way, he'd dedicated his existence to this one quest. Maybe he was chosen and this was where it should be.

That, or I'd been incarcerated too long and was becoming way too close to my captor. After all, what kind of man locks another up like this with such forethought? Not anybody you'd want to entrust the most powerful artifact in existence with, that was for sure.

Mind made up, and that meant I had to get the hell out of here before I did something stupid like decide he should have it, I leaned back on the bed and plotted my escape.

A week later and I was still plotting.

He'd also lost his mind completely now. A walking, ranting skeleton who clutched the box tight everywhere he went.

There was no more food, no more fresh water to wash with or to brush my teeth, just a bottle of water to drink when he remembered. The knots were back in my hair too, which annoyed me no end.

Time was running out for both of us. If he died with me trapped in here I'd follow along soon after. And I really didn't want to die. I knew what waited for me when I did. A very pissed off Death.

Hello Stranger

As I lay on my bed with my fingers laced together behind my head, a familiar tingle made things stir. With a mighty force of will, I rallied against such engorging, feeling dirty yet accepting it wasn't my fault—the fae will do it to you every time.

Faery dust fell inside my glass prison and I smiled. I got goosebumps, felt lightheaded, and my grin widened as the most perfect, and utterly disconcerting, not to mention terrifying, woman I had ever met, or anyone else had ever met for that matter, appeared in front of me.

This vision of loveliness, clad in a skintight green dress reaching halfway down shapely thighs, shook her curly golden locks and more faery dust fell, shimmering all the colors of the rainbow as it danced around the room. Magical motes of pure loveliness that each contained a beautiful dream if you ever managed to capture one, which was strictly not allowed on pain of excruciating death delivered by the angel that stood before me in her very high heels.

"My poor, beautiful human, why have they locked you up? Is that poo I smell?" asked Sasha, wrinkling her pert nose I found hard to stop staring at. I found myself ogling her ample bosom instead, squashed as it was inside her low cut dress like two excited puppies keen for release to come out and play. At the thought, I smiled and must have done something pervy with my tongue because Sasha snapped her fingers and said, "Hello? Face is up here," whilst my tongue flared red hot and I put it back inside my mouth where it belonged.

I lifted my gaze and stared into the sweet, smiling face of my faery godmother.

"Hello, Sasha, you couldn't have come at a better time. What took you so long?"

"I came as soon as I could, Arthur. You aren't an easy man to find. Do you know how big the desert is? And the sand, ugh! Horrible stuff." Sasha slapped her bottom, it jiggled.

"Need any help removing it?" I asked. Damn, what was with me? I was becoming a right perverted old man. Sasha gave me a strange look. "Hey, I've been locked up for weeks, and roaming this damn desert before that. I'm, ugh..."

"Horny?" she asked with a wry smile.

"I guess," I said, scratching at my beard. "Thought I'd be too weak, too out of sorts, but—"

"But you are a man, and you would think of sex even as you were being eaten alive by an alligator," she noted with a sad shake of the head.

"Yeah, we're all idiots, I know. Anyway," I said, excited, "have you come to rescue me?"

"I have come," she said, sitting beside me on the bed and crossing one flawless leg over the other. I couldn't stop staring at her kneecap. How could a kneecap be so damn perfect?

"Um, that wasn't actually an answer, you just made a statement."

"Indeed," she said, brushing imaginary lint from a bare shoulder.

"As evasive as ever," I noted. "So, how's things? Long time no see. Where you been?"

"Things are good. I kept my distance, tried not to interfere, as you were cross with me."

"That was ages ago. We've seen each other since then. You know I love you, even though you got me to sign a contract I have no memory of and now I have to be Death when I die."

"Oh, good, as long as you aren't holding a grudge."

"Me? The very idea." We smiled at each other. How could I remain cross with her? She'd given me so much, so many chances. "Love you."

"I love you too." We had a hug. Damn, it had been a while since I felt human contact like this. Or fae contact. Any contact.

"Now, how about you get me out of here? You are my faery godmother, after all."

"I'm afraid that isn't possible, Arthur," said Sasha sadly. "I cannot interfere in this."

"Why not? That's what you do best. Interfere. Help a poor wizard out, can't you?"

"I cannot. This is up to you. There is nothing I can do to help apart from offer you my support, a morale boost. Is it working?"

"Yeah, feeling awesome," I grumbled.

My host came dashing in, box clutched tight, and screamed, "Please open it. It's mine."

"Sorry, no can do, and besides, I have a guest."

He looked up from the box, took one look at Sasha, and ran screaming from the room.

"Something I said?" asked Sasha with a raised eyebrow.

"Nah, don't worry, he's like that with all the beautiful fae inside impenetrable glass prisons he made to trap unwary wizards."

"Oh good, that's all right then." Sasha smiled sweetly.

For a super-intelligent otherworldly being, she never did quite catch on to human sarcasm. Bless her.

Some Company

Sasha made herself comfortable by scooting up to the pillows and elbowing me until I gave her room. She sighed as she leaned back, our heads almost touching, then turned to stare at me with eyes both disconcerting by their depth of knowledge and power yet beautiful and innocent.

"Ah, it's nice to relax. I've been very busy lately."

"Yeah, lovely. What you been doing?" I asked to take my mind off things.

"The family home, you remember?"

"I remember all right."

"I decided it was time to bring it back to life. To make it a happy place rather than one so full of horrid memories. It's growing nicely."

"That's good," I said, already zoning out because if Sasha was sleepy then so was everyone else. "You moving in then?"

"I haven't decided yet. When I left that foul place I vowed never to return, but after the incident, I still felt connected to it. We shall see," she murmured.

"Good, that's good."

Now, I'm not saying that fae snore, and I'm certainly not saying for one moment that Sasha was snoring loudly beside me, and even if she was it would be a lovely sound, no, I'm just saying that if they did, and if she was, then it wasn't at all annoying and was quite lovely in fact.

Her rhythmic breathing calmed my frayed nerves after my host's appearance, and I relaxed. I'd been on edge ever since he lost the plot and stopped feeding me or changing the damn toilet, and the stink was getting to me. Whatever he'd set up to allow me to breathe inside this glass bubble seemingly didn't do too well with odor removal, so I was feeling kind of grossed-out.

Sasha's chest rose and fell in an utterly hypnotic way and for a lesser mortal it would have been tempting to lie there for hours watching it move and jiggle so it's a good job I was a mighty wizard capable of rising above such base things.

Eventually, I must have dozed off, as the next thing I knew, startled from dreams of wobbling mountains, was my mad jailer's face pressed up against the glass staring in utter disbelief mixed with horror at the sight of me and Sasha taking an afternoon doze in my prison. He banged on the glass with the box so I turned away and ignored him.

Sasha stirred from her slumber and smiled like an angel.

"Better?" I asked.

"Much, thank you. What is that silly little man doing?"

"Don't mind him, he's just gone crazy because he can't have the artifact."

"Oh. Now, Arthur, I'm sure I don't need to warn you about this being a very dangerous business. That if this falls into the wrong hands it will be the end of life here on earth, and that will have serious repercussions for the fae. We are connected, after all."

"I know. So why not help a guy out? I can look after it, but not from in here."

"Sorry, my love, but it's forbidden. You know the rules, how these things work."

"Actually, no, I don't. You fae are a complicated lot, who knows what convoluted rules you have about these things."

"Section 371 of volume 19 of the Code of Practice in Times of Imminent Human Armageddon Due to Artifacts of Merit Being at Risk of—"

"Yeah, yeah, whatever. So, no help?"

Sasha sat up and waved a hand over her hair which obeyed and fell into place perfectly. She straightened her dress, ignored the noise at the glass, and as she stood she said, "Sorry, but no." And with that she was gone.

Faery dust fell and I was alone once more.

Apart from the nutter squashing his face against the glass and ranting and raving.

Surely There's a Way?

My mental host sank to his knees, his face pushed tight against the glass, which must have hurt, but he was beyond that now, felt no pain, wouldn't even know it was happening.

He was consumed by the artifact, had thoughts only for it and the otherworldly delights it promised. True power, to harness such primordial forces, to conquer, destroy, or to work wondrous magic and make the world a better place, all were possible with the power it could unleash if used correctly by someone with vast magical experience and a level head.

Which was exactly why nobody should have it, as nobody is like that deep down. Everyone is screwed up in their own way and nobody should have that kind of responsibility or opportunity. It would drive you mad, and it had. This poor dude was the perfect example of why it should never, ever, be used. Just wanting it, craving it, and carrying the box, was enough to tip him over the edge. Sure, he must have been hovering close to the precipice anyway to lose the plot like this. All those years waiting had clearly consumed him, put him dangerously close to sliding into madness, but it was this closeness to the artifact, being so near yet so far from the actual item that had done for him in the end.

There were countless tales of the depths adepts had sunk to when under its thrall, how it affected the mind and body, let alone the stories about those who'd managed to hold the genuine article and try to uncover its true power.

It was limitless and it was extremely tempting to try to use it. It made the Gates of Bakaudif seem like a toy in comparison. This was a true portal to real magic, the serious kind that could transform the world and allow you to do pretty much anything. But the cost was too high, the risk too great, and the danger impossible to ignore. Heck, it was so important, so wondrous, that it didn't even have a name. Adepts throughout the ages had refused to name it as that would give it even more power. It was merely the first artifact, and you could capitalize it if you wanted, but superstition, and outright fear, stopped most from even doing that. Nobody, and I mean nobody, had ever succeeded in harnessing it and remaining sane, and as I watched the pitiful form curl up on the floor, clutching the box tight, I understood why my old master had been quite as nuts as he was.

He'd used it, or tried to, or had kept it near for too long and the result was a semi-madness that left him unstable, messed up in the head, yet still able to function in his own wild, erratic way. That's why he'd buried it so deep, kept it protected and safe, because he must have realized, and with a mighty force of will had done what was necessary to hide it from magical eyes.

So why the fuck did he make me uncover it?

Goddammit! Would his deception never end? Why did he want me to have it? Just because it was time for it to move on? Time for it to be hidden again somewhere deeper and darker, more secure? Guess so. It was the only answer I could come up with and the only answer I would ever get. He was dead and gone, at rest. Unlike this poor soul before me.

Later, as dusk fell, the shell of a man the other side of the glass clambered to his feet and pleaded with me all over again. He shrieked, he cried, he smiled a perverse smile and asked me nicely, but the answer remained the same.

"No."

He ran around the room, waving one arm then the other, never letting go of the box, and when he'd thoroughly exhausted himself he stopped suddenly like he'd slammed into the glass and just stood there, swaying.

"Look, any chance of a drink and food? I'm dying in here. Clean clothes and a shower would be nice too." I smiled at him sweetly, hoping to get a sensible response. He was still in there somewhere, I knew that, and if he'd just let go of the damn box he might even return to a semblance of normality. It was doubtful he'd ever be completely right again, but there was still hope if he'd just give up on his futile quest. Surely he knew I'd rather die than let him get his hands on it?

He came up close to the grill so I'd hear him properly and said, "Give it to me and you will be free."

"No."

He ran screaming from the room. I didn't see him again for three days.

Time's Running Out

When he returned, it was clear things would come to a head soon. He slipped a bottle of water through the hatch along with a few scraps and then it closed tighter than Vicky's ponytail, the seal utterly invisible and trust me, I'd tried to get it to open, he smiled apologetically before leaving without saying a word.

He looked better, had put on a little weight, even lost that manic look in his eyes, and seemed almost like his old self. He'd clearly come to terms with things and had accepted that there would be no easy way for him to get what he wanted. His madness had passed, or the outward manifestation of it anyway. What was going on inside his head was a different matter entirely.

The calm before the storm.

I knew there and then that if I didn't get out, and today, then something awful would happen. Something worse than being locked in a glass prison for nigh on three weeks.

By now I was weak, starving, and very thirsty. I gulped the water, ate the food, and tried not to breathe in deeply because the stink had become unbearable. Today, it had to be today. Either he would kill me or I'd die soon from neglect. He'd forget to feed me again, forget water, and it would be the end of me.

Reluctantly, and knowing I was playing a dangerous game, I sat cross-legged on the bed, ignored the filthy sheets, and centered myself. My mind emptied, my senses blocked to external stimuli, and I became still inside. All that remained was magic. Magic born of years of practice, magic I had harnessed countless times, true power direct from the Quiet Place combined with my own innate nature that took hold and became my entire existence.

I was magic, I had it inside me, and I let it all build up, to focus and become as potent as it ever had.

My will grew as tightly focused as a laser beam, a single pinpoint of clarity that expanded and hardened, compressed even as it became larger, until I felt it like a physical lump in my throat that began to force its way out of my mouth. No, this wasn't what I wanted, so I concentrated, pictured the magic traveling down into my chest then along my arm until it reached my elbow.

Slowly, and carefully, I slid Wand from his resting place where he had remained for many weeks now. I knew if I'd got him involved earlier I would have lost my mind, as sitting in a cell talking to a stick is not the best way to keep sane.

Now I needed him, and he needed me, so I pulled him out, said, "Ssh, no talking," and he dipped his head silently in reply.

He knew what I wanted, and wasted no time.

With a grunt, I let magic spasm down my arm and the connection was made. He lit up like a Christmas tree and the sigils shone in all their glory along his shaft, first in sequence, then in ways to make spells manifest that had lain dormant since imbued into his essence.

He spat them all forth at once, gave it everything he had, and fiery magic more volatile than anything I had ever used before shot from his tip and collided with the glass with all my will, all my strength, all my magic behind it.

The magic spread like a flame against the glass until a whole wall was ablaze as it tried to chew through and break down the wards simultaneously. I focused harder, so hard my whole body shook, yet still the glass held and the wards remained unchanged. With a shout that tore at my parched throat I redoubled my efforts and Wand burned hot in my hand as he channeled my will and increased it tenfold.

The magic shone fierce purple as it lapped against the glass, searching for a weakness, any hint of a way to break me free from my prison.

I felt the change, felt the magic flow through the tiniest of gaps. Through the blaze I saw the magic slide through the outline where the hatch was. This was a weakness, a break in the seal that had to be beefed up more than the other wards for it to remain tamper-proof. Maybe he'd been lax, maybe my magic was just powerful enough, but I didn't care and just kept on pushing, tightening the focus until everything pointed at the hairline fracture.

Magic burned bright and clawed at the lines of the hatch then broke free and spread out on the other side of the glass. It pounded away, searching for a way to wear the wards down enough for the glass to crack under the pressure, and I was winning. The magic spread on the outside of my prison with disconcerting intensity.

A rug caught fire on the floor and flames, real flames, erupted, incinerating the wool. Sparks flew and in an instant wall hangings, the furniture, and then the walls and ceiling were burning.

The man ran into the room, eyes wide, then was forced back as it became a raging inferno. I felt nothing. The wards had held, my magic waned, and I watched as the house burned around me.

For an hour I sat there, watching. My magic was spent and Wand was already asleep without us exchanging a word. The room burned until I could see the bare structure of the building, then the timber frames broke and the roof collapsed. Brittle, dry wood in the heat of Africa was an incendiary time bomb, and I'd just let it off.

When the smoke finally cleared I found myself sitting on a bed inside a glass cage, staring at the ashes of the building. I had a clear view of the garden and the desert beyond. Everything was burned. The grass was gone along with the rest of the garden, the building was nothing but charred wood, and there, off in the distance silhouetted by the setting sun, was the man responsible for this madness.

He looked like he was howling at the moon. Maybe he was.

Getting Desperate

One thing I hadn't paid much, make that any, attention to whilst incarcerated was the temperature. The bedroom was surprisingly cool throughout the day and somewhat chilly but not uncomfortably so at night. That was when it was inside the house.

Outside was a whole different matter.

As the mad old man wailed, yanked at his hair one-handed, and ran to and fro around the remains of his life's work, now nothing but scorched earth and smoldering piles, I came to realize that I had done a very foolish thing. I was exposed to the temperatures of the desert.

The air cooled at an alarming rate as night took hold and we were plunged into darkness, nothing but the embers of a man's dreams offering weak patches of light. I watched as he danced around the ruins, casting long shadows as he picked though the ruined pieces of a lifetime of collecting and organizing a home for himself. There was nothing left as far as I could tell.

I was spent, utterly exhausted in a way I felt I would never recover from, with only my hat and a sleeping Wand for company. Without the fortifying mixture of water and food, I was unable to fight off the encroaching cold that sank deep into my bones and set my teeth to chattering. I curled up under the blankets and closed my eyes to the madness that was undoubtedly going on around me and snuggled deep, searching for warmth.

My body heat offered little comfort even under the blankets but at least I had a comfortable bed to be unhappy on.

With there being nothing I wanted to see, my eyes remained firmly shut until a hint of the morning sun forced me from under the covers. It was only then that I could appreciate the true extent of the carnage I had wrought in my attempt to escape this nightmare.

He was asleep the other side of the glass, the ever-present box clutched tight to his chest as he whimpered and twitched, deep in the throes of a nightmare I still couldn't bring myself to believe he truly deserved. He was a lost soul, had wasted a life searching for something that would never bring happiness, only misery, and I felt for him even after all he'd done.

There had been enough killing and I didn't want him dead. Only to be free of his grasp and on my way. I doubted it would end without one of us dying though —it sure as shit wouldn't be me.

The sun rose, the piles of timber burned, the grass was black, and so was my mood.

I upended the empty water bottle and managed to get a few drops, but it wasn't enough. I doubted there could ever be enough water to quench my raging thirst.

It grew hot, then hotter still, and I questioned how come I hadn't felt the heat of the fire yet felt the heat of the sun. Must be the way the wards had been set up. Constructed to protect against unforeseen accident yet not to battle with the outside temperature under natural conditions. Just my luck. I'd survived a raging inferno but I'd be steamed alive in what now amounted to a very well constructed greenhouse.

My tormentor twitched then slowly woke from his dreams. He stood on shaky legs, glanced at me, then turned away and surveyed the carnage of his life.

He mewled, hung his head, and wandered off to inspect the damage. Don't know why, it was obvious it was all gone, nothing left.

I shouted for him, banged on the glass, but all it brought was sweat and pain. Exhausted, I collapsed onto the bed and lay there, panting, wondering how long it would take for me to be roasted alive.

Reluctantly, not wishing to expend the energy, I stripped down to my underwear and stood, swaying, unable to remain upright without resting my palms on the glass. Bad move. It was boiling already, and it was still only mid-morning. By the afternoon I would be dead, so I had to come up with another, and much better, plan, and soon.

Baked Wizard

Through slitted eyes, I watched the man wander across the dead grass and into the desert proper. He ambled, as if in no hurry. I wondered if I'd ever see him again. My heart sank as he crowned a rise then disappeared down the other side. I kept my eyes trained on his last location and was mighty relieved when he reappeared and stood there, staring back at the ruins.

What a strange sight it must have made. A large glass box sitting surrounded by the remains of his home, and I laughed because of the absurdity of it all.

Sweat ran from every pore and I was soaked through, already panting. Things were getting desperate and I was well aware of how little time I had left. I had to escape but I didn't know how.

He remained where he was, just stared, and I banged and shouted but to no avail. Maybe he had returned to his madness, surely this was enough to push him totally over the edge? Maybe he was perfectly sane and had accepted he would never get what he wanted from me so would leave me to die. Or maybe he didn't see me at all, had forgotten. Maybe he simply didn't care.

The sun rose higher, the temperature along with it, and I used what little magic remained to amp up Grace to the max. It cooled my head, allowed thoughts to form, and I decided that if nothing else I needed to stuff as much magic inside myself as I could if for no other reason than to die with a cool head. So I looked inward, went to the Quiet Place, and sank deeply into the cold, uncaring embrace of a frigid universe.

When I emerged, it was to unbearable heat and terrible humidity. I was brimming with magic but empty of ideas, and I knew it was futile to go for a repeat of yesterday and try to escape by brute force.

I searched the horizon for the man only to find him running back towards me. Was he about to release me? Had he had a change of heart? My heart leapt as he ran fast but then he fell, stumbled on a steaming mound and it was then I saw what he'd been running from.

Two men, clad in lightweight gear for the desert, coupled with substantial backpacks and each holding aloft long, gnarled staffs.

Wizards!

Guess the artifact had been calling out, disturbing the magical fields enough for them to finally hone in on it. My wards still held, but they must have searched the area and the damn fire would have given us away.

The air flared with streaks of magic as their staffs let loose a torrent of destruction aimed at the man, but it washed over him as if he had a forcefield protecting him. Neat. Guess he was a wizard after all. He stood, then turned to face them, shouting and waving an arm and pointing, telling them to leave. They hollered something back, shook their heads, then attacked again with the same ineffective result.

My jailer laughed, a sound that carried across the emptiness to me, and it definitely wasn't the laugh of anyone sane.

He pointed again but they merely angled their staffs at him and let rip.

The magic tore at the already ravaged earth, whipped up a storm of ash and sparks but he remained unaffected. He strode forward and they retreated several steps then spoke quickly to each other before splitting up. Both ran then stopped when they faced him from opposite sides.

With a nod, each set forth a volley of dark magic that hit him simultaneously. He disappeared behind a cloud of smoke and molten sand.

Guess it was out of the frying pan and into the fire for yours truly.

Earth Shattering

Sweat poured into my eyes even as Grace worked her hardest. My whole body was drenched and, perversely, I became cleaner than I had for days. As foul grime was sluiced from my emaciated flesh, I stood in a puddle of my own filth and watched events unfold, unable to have any fun of my own.

As the ash blew away so the man was revealed. He stood there, cradling the box, untouched by the best the two rogue wizards could throw at him. He was blackened by soot, his clothes were scorched in places, but he was uninjured. He laughed as the two men approached warily, closing in on him from both sides. They faltered, unsure what to do with this strange specimen of a human being, and I didn't blame them.

Sound was cut off from me as they argued, pointing at the box as the old dude clutched it tighter. And then he did the damnedest thing. He actually placed it on the ground then stood erect and pointed at it, daring them to come get it.

No sooner had his lips stopped moving than they were racing towards him, unable to resist the lure of the artifact.

The man was utterly calm as he let his hands drop to his sides. He spread his fingers wide and lifted his hands slightly until they were parallel to the floor. I watched, mesmerized, as silver magic sparkled at his fingertips. He rose up, feet leaving the ground, as the magic grew until it disturbed the ground beneath him. Ash and sand swirled manically like he was powered by jets as he rose higher, and then in one swift motion he snapped his arms up and pointed a gnarled finger at each approaching wizard.

Forked magic shot from spasming hands and arced towards the men. Each raised a staff and blocked the assault but it was clearly powerful as they were both hurled away to land on their backs.

Not about to give up, they ran away from the man then turned to face him, meaning I got a good look at them. Men in their fifties, trained wizards unafraid of combat, battle-ready and experienced in fighting. These were wizards for hire, men who traveled, working for anyone who would pay them, performing tasks others were unable, or unwilling, to perform.

They closed ranks and tapped their staffs together forming a cross, then pointed them at the man so only the tips touched. I saw their lips move as they readied the spell, then the staffs burned bright and their combined magic spewed from the ends of the magical wood in a single tight beam of concentrated magic I knew would do for the old guy and leave me no better off, probably much worse.

Time slowed as the dark volley shot through the air aiming right at him, and it looked like it was all about to be over. A moment before the magic hit, the wily dude spun aside, the strike missing by a fraction. I watched, wide-eyed, yet unable to do anything, as it headed straight for me.

The magic hit like the wet splash of a balloon full of water dropped from a great height as the power erupted all around the glass prison. Every side was engulfed in black magic that screamed at me, a shockwave that penetrated the defenses of the wards and pierced my skull like a train screeching on dry tracks.

My whole world became nothing but noise and I covered my soaked ears with my hands as the intensity grew.

Boom!

The world shattered into a million pieces as glass rained down from above and thousands of shards exploded inward and upward. It tore at my flesh, jagged little barbs that left me covered in tiny cuts and embedded with glass.

As shocked and awed as I was, I wasted no time and grabbed my backpack from the floor. I stuffed my clothes inside, hastily slipped on jeans and boots, pushing shards of glass further into my flesh, then darted across the ground to rescue the box.

Too late! The man descended rapidly and grabbed it before he sent a rapid series of volleys at the two wizards that engulfed them in white light and burst the ground open all around them.

As sand and ash blew in all directions he ran off.

There was nothing else for it, I'd have to follow him, catch him before I lost him.

With a look over my shoulder, it was clear the two wizards weren't seriously harmed and would be after him soon enough, so I ignored the stabbing of the glass and gave chase.

At least that's what I would have liked to do, but I'd forgotten that I was as weak as a kitten, had hardly used my legs for weeks, and was in serious pain. I stumbled, then sprawled out on my stomach, as helpless as a newborn.

Ever had one of those days? I have.

No Way

Not about to be left behind while the most important item in magic land was whisked away and possibly soon thereafter fell into the hands of other nasty wizards, I pushed up and got to my feet, refusing to give in. I shook my legs to get some life into them, then took tentative steps before picking up speed as my muscles grew accustomed to moving again. No way, not ever, I didn't give up.

Such were my good intentions. The reality was something very different. With all of my mighty will, I was unable to move faster than a pensioner after double hip surgery. The mind was willing, the body gave me the finger. I pushed and pushed, forced my legs to move, to power up and give chase, but they refused point blank and just stumbled through the sand like I was walking on stilts.

I was a mess and no mistake. The once frisky Hat was ruined, unable to muster anything above a gentle walk. I plowed on regardless, gave chase to a man who had already disappeared. Knowing there was little time

and that the other two guys would be here in a
moment, I just did my best and put one foot in front of
the other. The more I walked, the looser the muscles
became, until the spring slowly returned to my step. I
found a rhythm, my own peculiar version of the true
desert walk, and I focused on that, let everything else
fade away. I got into my groove and stuck with it. Each
step moved me away from this strange ruined home
and further into the desert. Not that we'd gone far,
mind you, I'd only just managed to climb the slight rise
where the thief had disappeared, so it wasn't like I
wandered off too far.

Staring down onto the flat expanse of desert that
spread out in all directions, I sighed. Hell, if he headed
off into the wilderness we'd both be dead soon, if the
two other guys didn't kill us first.

Where was he? How could he disappear when
there was nowhere to hide?

There was no sign of him whatsoever. He'd
vanished off the face of the earth. He must be hiding,
but where? I glanced behind only to discover the two
wizards-for-hire were getting themselves together.
They'd had a good hiding, and would be feeling pretty
crappy, but you don't come this far and give up after
getting a few bruises, and they didn't seem like the type
to just walk away and call it quits. Where was my
bloody box? Where was the artifact? Where was the
demented old guy?

I followed the footsteps in the sand and headed
down into the desert. The sun was hot, I didn't have my
shirt on, and shreds of glass made every step torture. It

would have to wait, no time to stop and prise the splinters out or do anything but keep going. Head down, I traced his steps across the desert and then they stopped, just stopped. Confused, I looked around, even checked there wasn't anything above me he could've climbed, shaking my head while I did so because of course there wasn't. Well, if he didn't go up, then he must have gone down.

I stomped on the sand with my boot and wasn't surprised to find it was hollow. I bent and found that sand had been glued to something, presumably a trap door. There was a flat ring set into the door so I prised it up and lifted the hatch. Lights were on, there was a ladder, and there was no time to think about what I was doing so I climbed in, pulled the hatch closed behind me, and continued the chase.

Hopefully, he wouldn't be waiting at the bottom with something sharp to poke me nastily with. If he had any sense he'd be long gone, but he didn't have any sense, so I was nervous as hell as I climbed down the short ladder and only breathed when I stepped off into a narrow tunnel.

With a shrug, I followed the lights.

Sneaky

"The sneaky bugger," I said with a whistle as I emerged from the tunnel a few seconds later into what can only be described as, because it was, a large garage. A large double door was already open at the other end, revealing a ramp leading up and out.

Several trucks sat idle, the walls were lined with racks holding fuel cans, water, food, and numerous spare parts for the vehicles, plus all the usual crap you'd expect in a garage-cum-workshop. So this was where he hid away all the work stuff he'd used to build the house. He owned power tools galore, a generator, and lots of woodworking stuff.

It was a swanky underground garage any man would be proud to own. Hell, many would move in.

A gleaming truck revved, spewing noxious fumes into the garage before being sucked away by automated ducts in the ceiling, and then the truck screeched as it careened up the ramp and disappeared.

I ran to the nearest vehicle, found the keys in the glove compartment, along with a large amount of cash in a white envelope, so it was game on. I hurriedly grabbed anything I thought would be useful, focus on food, water, and fuel, threw most into the back, put copious rations on the passenger seat, got in, started it up first time, and followed the thief out of the garage.

Daylight hit with all its demented power and I was momentarily blinded. As my vision returned, I saw the truck careen towards the ruined house and right at the two wizards. They ran for all they were worth as the truck bore down, narrowly missing being flattened. I gave chase, even waved as we passed, then floored it and tried to catch the rogue old man and the box that could change the entire world if he somehow managed to open it. I knew he would, given time and the chance to disassemble the wards. Sure, it might take him a while, many months, but if he didn't go so mad that he couldn't keep himself alive then I had no doubt that sooner or later he, or someone else, would unlock the box and then I didn't want to think about what would happen.

Nothing is secure forever, and something like this, well, somebody would find a way.

I put my foot down and chased the dust. There was no hiding place out here, and I had every confidence I would catch him eventually. While I drove after him, I greedily drank water and devoured the food. As the chase continued, my energy levels rose as the snacks worked their magic. Ah, there's nothing like a sugar surge after starving for days. You forget what it's like to have the rush, to believe you might survive. Food is the true magic, better than anything, when you've been refused it for so long. Yet I was on a continent that battled with such issues constantly. My plight was as nothing compared to the millions who knew true hunger from the day they came into the world unto the day they left feeling just as empty inside.

So I put my woes into perspective and acknowledged how lucky I was to be in the position I was. Sure, I'd had a hard time of it, but I was alive, I had food, I even had a bloody vehicle. Things may have been dire, I may have been covered in glass and at my lowest point, but plenty had it much worse. Time to think positive. Time to get my box back. And time to get the hell out of Africa.

I kept following and he kept driving fast and expertly through the desert. He knew how to handle the terrain better than me, and his speed was disconcerting. No way would I normally drive so fast across such unstable ground. It may have looked flat, but the desert was no place to get carried away. There were countless hidden holes filled with loose sand, or rocks, or dips that could trash the wheels, tear the axle, do untold damage. Yet my quarry seemed to either disregard such concerns or wasn't concerned at all.

I tried to keep up but he was getting away, no matter how hard I tried. I was bounced around the cab until I grew concerned for the safety of my spine. The jolts sent sharp pains into my lumbar region until I felt unable to keep up the speed for genuine fear of doing irreversible damage. But if he could do it then so could I, so I gritted my teeth, added it to the growing list of things to moan about, and did my best to match his speed.

No matter how hard I tried, I simply couldn't continue, and just when I was contemplating slowing to a less bone-breaking speed we hit the road leading to the main town. It was a good ways off, he'd told me that, but the going was easier and my bottom thanked me for the opportunity to recover. The moment we hit the smoother, well-worn if still very dodgy compacted surface, my quarry really went for it. He kicked up a cloud of dust and sped off, leaving me in his wake.

The fine sand was so thick it completely clouded my vision, leaving me driving by guesswork alone. I eased back so we had some distance between us and this allowed me to at least see where I was going. Keeping the same distance, I followed his trail and kept on following, refusing to give up, refusing to give in to the terrible state I was in, and refusing to even contemplate losing him.

If he made it to the town and did a runner he could be gone for good and I'd have the mother of all jobs tracking him down.

My wards were good, and I could follow them, but just as they didn't give a precise location to anyone trying to track the artifact, it left me in exactly the same boat. If he disappeared I might never find him again, which didn't bear thinking about.

Civilization

As if from nowhere, the world changed. From following the dust trail of the truck in front for miles through the blistering desert heat, the landscape morphed. Houses lined the road, people were everywhere, and cars, bikes, scooters, and every kind of vehicle imaginable were suddenly vying for space on the dirt.

The center of town was up ahead, no more than a mile away, and through the open window I could hear the hustle and bustle of thousands of people going about their business, struggling for survival, doing whatever it took to put food on their table.

It was overwhelming and I hadn't even reached the heart of the town yet, but it was such a welcome sight at the same time. You could easily believe you were one of the last remaining people alive when you were out in the desert. That everything you'd experienced before, all the people, the sounds, the sights, were a figment of your imagination. That all there really was, all that endured, was sand and heat.

And yet here I was, heading back to people and commerce, traffic and fumes, noise and the cruel vagaries of human nature. Glorious.

I weaved in and out of traffic, getting desperate, but I kept him in my sights and ignored the honking of horns and the crazy driving all around me. Nobody followed any road rules, drove on whatever side they felt like, cut across you and shouted, as if you were in the wrong, but we made progress and headed into the heart of the town. It wasn't a large place, more an outpost than anything, but it still held many thousands of people. Easily enough roads, alleys, and paths to get lost in, to hide from a desperate wizard who wanted nothing more than to go home and lie in his bed for a thousand years or so. Once I'd got the glass out, of course.

Thinking it best to look presentable, if not smell it, I slipped a stinking shirt over my sweat-soaked, bruised, bleeding body, and continued to if not give chase then at least meander through the bustling streets. A market was in full cacophonous effect, stalls everywhere, people bartering for all they were worth with smiles on their faces, and we eased through it all, him three vehicles ahead, then five, then two as other cars took side roads. I dared not risk getting out and approaching on foot in case he did something stupid like plow through pedestrians. He was desperate, and was liable to overreact, as he surely knew I was behind him.

Speaking of which, the one thing I'd studiously ignored until now were the two mercenary wizards who'd been trailing me the whole time. Just as I was following the old man's dust, so they were following mine, and they were just as persistent. Another reason to not risk it on foot. They might try to intercept me whilst I did the same to the guy in front.

So we played a slow game of cat and mouse, or were we all mice, or all cats? However it worked, none of us risked being caught by the other or trying to make a run for it on foot. We inched through the madness. I ignored people trying to sell me fruit and several live chickens held up to the open window, my scowl of annoyance enough to send them away, but secretly I was enjoying the noise and the affirmation that I wasn't one of the last human beings alive.

This was wonderful after my incarceration and I wished I could have taken the time to enjoy the sounds, sights, and smells the bazaar had to offer in spades, but my attention was on one thing, and one thing only.

Caught unawares, despite me thinking I was focused, the way ahead was clear as the market ended and my quarry wasted no time flooring his truck and taking a fast right turn at a junction. I shouted at the man dangling a bunch of bananas through the window then put my foot down and closed the window despite the heat.

I took the turn and noted with dismay tinged with hope that he was heading for the small airport. Haha, no way would he be lucky enough to get a plane out of here before I could catch up with him. Right?

No Fair

There are rules for flying, even when the plane you are about to catch is tiny and twice your age. Even when it's an internal flight and a short one at that. You still have to go through check in, you still have to show your passport or ID, and you still have to be stared at blankly by someone who will shoot you if they think you've got a bottle of water.

Of course, if you're a demented old man carrying the most important artifact in the world and you have one wizard after you who you've locked up for weeks in a magical glass cage and two other violent wizards you've just had a barney with, you could always take the more unconventional route.

As I followed him through the chain-link fence he'd just flattened and chased him across the tarmac, it was obvious which route this particular wizard had chosen.

He skidded to a halt and jumped from the truck, clutching the box to his chest. A backpack fell heavily over his shoulders. The people queuing to board the plane glanced around then ignored him and filed inside. Maybe this was common practice in these here parts.

He had a quick word with one of the stewards and an envelope was given, and then he rushed onto the plane. Aha, the old bribery trick.

I pulled up beside his vehicle and grabbed my gear and the envelope from the glove box that now made perfect sense then hurried to the plane, every step hurting more than the last. The stewardess was closing the rear door so I took the steps two at a time and yelled for her to wait. She took one glance at me and tried to close up in a hurry. Not surprising, as I would have looked a right state, and she could probably smell me too. I know I was making myself feel ill from the pong.

I rifled through the envelope of cash then just shoved the whole thing into her hands and said, "Take it all. I have to catch this flight." She looked at me dubiously, then at the stack of cash, and nodded reluctantly.

"Please stay away from the other passengers. You may wash once we have taken off." She held her nose and stepped aside to let me board.

I nodded my thanks then hurried onto the plane and took a seat close to the exit; there were plenty to choose from.

The old dude was up near the front, sitting at a window seat looking out onto the runway. He craned his neck as shouts could be heard from outside and then I turned to look behind me at the fuss. The two wizards stepped cautiously down the aisle. They spotted me but kept on walking then spoke quietly when they spied the guy upfront.

I expected it all to kick off there and then, but instead they took their seats next to each other halfway up the plane.

They watched the old guy, I watched the old guy and them watching him, and the man with all the prizes steadfastly refused to turn around but kept his eyes forward and his head down.

The usual warning about it being likely we would all die mid-air came over the tannoy and then we were taxiing down the runway. Ten seconds later we were in the sky and I was contemplating just how it was possible for such a small, ancient, battered metal machine to remain airborne. Damn but I hated flying, and this promised to be one of the least fun flights yet. At least it would be a quick flight.

Not Now

The stewardess did the rounds, asking if we wanted drinks or snacks. At the exorbitant prices, it was no wonder nobody bought a thing. Instead, and as was the norm, people pulled out their own provisions and soon there was a rather epic picnic in progress.

The passengers laughed and joked amongst themselves, shared food with neighbors and generally had a great old time of it. Except for four men who weren't part of the party. We were left alone, clearly outsiders or too rude to be made part of Team Scary Flight, so whilst everyone tucked in and had fun, we spent our time eyeing each other up and wondering who would make the first move.

After an hour, my eyelids grew heavy and I began to nod off. I stretched my legs in the aisle and made use of the cramped bathroom, having a wash as best I could in the ridiculously confined space. It wasn't pretty, it wasn't pleasant, but at least I removed most of the glass.

Back in my seat, I munched on my own snacks and tried to think how best to approach this. Should I go batter the demented old fool over the head and take what was mine by right of me having it before him? Would he cause trouble if I did? Of course he would, and so would the other two guys, if they even let me get that far.

What then? A full-on mid-flight magic-fest somewhere over the desert? I didn't fancy being another statistic, like the plane that had nearly done for me in the desert. So, I should just wait it out, hold back until we were in Dire Dawa and then clobber him and run off laughing, that was the sensible thing to do.

The two up front kept turning to check on me, and the man we were all after kept his head down and rocked back and forth in his chair. How lost a soul was he? Had he recovered enough to have a plan, or was he winging it? His escape hinted that he knew exactly what he'd been doing, and I wondered if all of it had been an act and he was as sane as he ever was. Maybe he'd been playing for sympathy, or maybe he thought I'd fear for my life if I saw him go nuts and give him what he wanted in the mistaken belief I could retrieve it from a madman easily enough. Or maybe he was smart and insane.

Did it matter? Not really, no, but it's always good to understand your opponent. Nobody likes the unforeseen, and I was utterly in the dark about this man. A wizard, and a powerful one, willing to wait patiently for years to get what he wanted wasn't to be trifled with, and he wasn't to be underestimated. Guess the two mercenaries were as loath as me to start anything mid-air, as they made no sign of trying to approach him, and that was good.

I jolted awake to the stewardess shoving at my shoulder whilst trying to stay as far away from me as possible.

"We will be arriving in fifteen minutes, sir, please fasten your seatbelt."

I nodded and moved to do as I was told.

"Motherfuckers," I growled, already out of my seat as the two men surged forward as everyone else, including the man with the best box in town, buckled up.

"Sirs, please, back in your seats," screeched the panicked stewardess, but they paid her no mind.

The two men stormed up the aisle one behind the other, and at the sound of the stewardess the old dude turned. He took me back with the look on his face. He was calm, almost serene, and unperturbed by the men mere steps away.

As they reached him and lifted their staffs, something not uncommon on African flights, although it bloody well should be as large sticks and confined spaces do not mix, so the old man flung up his arms and they were shunted back with a force-nine gale that every other passenger felt. He unbuckled himself and slid across the seats then stood in the aisle, the box under one arm, his other pointing at the men.

"Do not risk your lives and everyone else's aboard. You know what I have and that it is worth risking death for. I will do what it takes to secure it, and if you get in my way I will destroy you." He looked past them and stared right at me. He knew I was here all along but this was the first time he'd acknowledged it.

"Hi," I said, waving.

"Hello, Arthur. This could have been so easy."

"Yeah, if you'd played fair. Some host."

"Needs must, dear boy. I thought you would take pity on me and give me what I wanted, loosen your grip somewhat, but you are a wily fellow."

"Not as wily as you. Oh, by the way, what's your name?"

"There is power in names, I will not give you mine. You may call me what you wish, but you will not get my birth name."

"Suit yourself. How about Desert Rat?"

"As you wish. It means little to me. Will you risk the lives of innocents too, Arthur?"

I glanced around at the shocked passengers. "No, absolutely not."

The two wizards scrambled to their feet and magic crackled as their staffs burned bright. "But I can't say the same for them."

"A shame," he said, before he did the damnedest thing and lunged for the nearest window. His palm slapped against the thick plastic they use to stop you being sucked out of a very small gap and as it did so I saw a flash of silver.

Then the plastic blew out, the air pressure along with it, and everyone screamed as masks dropped from above and people frantically tried to get them over their faces before they suffocated. I wasn't exactly sure what would happen with the cabin de-pressurizing, but I assumed it wouldn't be something good. So as my ears popped I plonked myself back down in my seat, put my seatbelt on, and reached for my mask.

It blew in all directions, hanging as it was by a fragile cord, and that right there is a serious design flaw. As I clawed at it, my breath gone, I felt the weight of the world rush to my head as the plane lurched and my guts tried their hardest to punch out through my ears.

Justified Nervousness

"And this is why I hate flying," I grumbled to nobody as everyone was preoccupied freaking out and trying to get hold of their masks.

My head pounded from the change in pressure, my lungs burned, and I couldn't help gasping for air like a fish out of water. Finally, I got hold of the damn mask and breathed deeply several times to calm my frayed nerves, then reluctantly hopped out of my seat and moved cautiously down the aisle, grabbing seats for support, and helped people use their masks as I went while I held my breath.

Passengers nodded their gratitude as they took in deep lungfuls of air and I even buckled in a few kids whose parents' hands were too shaky.

Halfway down the aisle, the plane lurched violently as the numpties up ahead waged magical warfare in a tin box hurtling through the air. Sparks crackled, the air alive with the smell of magic, and it was all I could do to remain upright.

With a sigh, I released the Velcro from my very grubby combats and pulled out an excited Wand.

"Can you calm these fuckwits down?" I asked.

"Am I brown and sticky?"

"You sure are, buddy. Nothing dangerous," I warned. "There are citizens aboard and we don't want any causalities."

"You got it, but it would be much easier if I could just blast their heads off or pop a few eyeballs."

"You know that talk I keep saying we need to have?"

"Yeah?"

"We definitely need to have it. You have an unhealthy preoccupation with eyeballs."

"I am you, you are me," said Wand smugly.

"Yeah, yeah, just sort them out." I felt my will surge and the familiar tremor in my arm as magic coursed through my energy lines. My hand warmed as Wand flared into joyous true life, an existence beyond comprehension, a life so strange yet wondrous. He absorbed and channeled my intent, my wishes, my will, and the magic that joined us together burst forth with a tight focus that saved any unfortunate eyeball popping before it hit its mark with utter precision.

Poor guy didn't really stand a chance. Both wizards were facing towards the man we all wanted a chat with so he didn't see it coming. Neither did the other guy, who got hit in the head a moment later by a second round of brief fire from Wand's glowing tip.

The magic infused in the spell that ceased being a spell of words and intonation many years ago, now merely a brief thought I'm sure Wand forced me to have, hit each with enough power to fry their heads from the inside out. Their brains boiled to incredible temperatures in a steam bath even the Turk couldn't manage at Satan's Breath, and they slumped to the ground, very dead, very steamy. Their staffs clattered onto the threadbare carpet and the magic within them died.

"What did I just say?" I asked Wand with a sigh.

"Nothing about boiling brains being a bad idea," he said with post-magic satisfaction. If he'd asked for a cigarette I wouldn't have been surprised.

The old man nodded his thanks as we locked eyes. I blew on Wand's tip then stashed him away, sure he'd return to action soon enough.

The plane dove sharply and I was knocked off my feet along with a stewardess and several passengers. I cracked my head on a padded armrest that still had the little ashtray embedded. Ah, those were the days. Damn, when did I last have a smoke? Weeks ago. Maybe now would be a good time to quit. Maybe now would be an even better time to take it up in earnest.

As I clambered to my feet, I knew something was seriously wrong. The plane was lurching this way and that even as we descended, and I knew the old guy was responsible. He didn't trust me after this, believed I'd try something now the plane was in uproar. He couldn't have been more wrong. I wouldn't risk the lives of citizens like that. I'd bide my time and boil his head when we were alone.

Can't say I wasn't tempted though. If I'd been closer to him, if there weren't so many people up ahead all panicking and shouting at the stewardess, if I could have been certain I'd hit my mark and the old guy wouldn't retaliate and kill an innocent then yeah, I would have killed him there and then.

The plane banked and I stumbled forward down the aisle. He panicked and ran to the front of the plane, thinking I was about to attack.

He glanced back at me and I shouted, "No," but it was too late. He placed his hand on the small door with a green EXIT sign above and magic flared into the door. It glowed white around the seal and then flung open to the sound of screeching metal above the roar of air in the cabin.

I shook my head, telling him no, but he searched around frantically as he gripped the door frame. Lockers flew open to movement of his hand and a parachute slid across the floor. He grabbed it, and without even strapping it on he jumped out of the damn plane.

Frantic, I ran forward, shoving people aside as gently as I could, then I jumped out after him.

In hindsight, it was a somewhat foolish thing to do. And yet I smiled a smug smile as I hurtled towards the ground at way too many miles an hour. I always knew airplanes were dangerous, and I was right.

I tumbled arse over head through the warm air, but regained dubious control by tucking my arms against my sides. Now I was an arrow shooting through space, aiming right at my target. An old man clutching a box, trying to figure out how to put on a parachute whilst plummeting to certain death.

The ground got alarmingly close and I changed my angle somewhat to intercept the old guy but I misjudged it and shot past him, certain to be dead within seconds.

Good Save

Beyond panicked, I fumbled Wand out of my pocket and we wasted no time getting down to business. With one hand, I pointed him straight out, then curled into a ball, somersaulted, then went rigid as a board as my feet were facing down. Wand burst into life, spreading a wide disc of diffuse energy beneath me, offering a cushion of air that slowed progress a little.

It wasn't much, but it was enough to allow the crazy old dude to catch up with me. As he passed, I reached out and grabbed him by the crook of his arm, and then I drew him in close and hugged him tight whilst still using Wand to battle against gravity.

We were going to hit, and hard, so I took a risk and used my Wand hand to hook over the strap of the parachute. Wand burned through the cord holding the parachute inside and then the whole thing was released. For one terrible moment I thought we would hit before the parachute deployed. I watched as the cord extended and then there was a mighty tug as the canopy opened and we were yanked skyward. That's what it felt like, anyway. Obviously, we were still falling, but the upward drag made it feel like we were shooting up rather than down, which suited me just fine.

I gripped the mad dude tight with my arm, my shoulder screamed with the weight, but he did the sensible thing and gripped on with one arm, still unwilling to release the box. We spiraled and spun, flew sideways as we squirmed under the parachute, and I feared we would become tangled and the chute wouldn't work. Should I release him? It would certainly ensure my own survival. Would the box be okay? It should be, but was I willing to take the risk?

Goddammit!

I kept hold of him, partly because of the box, but also because I didn't want to kill him. Not really. Okay, maybe a little, maybe a lot. He'd sure put me through the wringer and no mistake. But there was just something about him that stopped me opting to end his sorry life. Maybe the fact I could feel the magic coursing through his arm had something to do with it. I got the sneaking suspicion that if I released him he'd blast me, and blast me good, before using his magic to save himself.

We drifted down then landed with one hell of a bump.

The parachute dragged us across the ground in a tangle of limbs, rope, backpacks, and boxes. The wind was gentle but there was breeze enough to catch the chute and we continued to be pulled across the rough ground in the middle of nowhere. Visions of being flayed alive by rocks clouded my mind, and wouldn't that be bloody typical. After everything I'd been through, after falling from an airplane and actually surviving, I get killed by the desert after all.

I dug my heels in and he had sense enough to do the same. Finally we came to a stop.

"Are you mad?" I shouted into his face as I untangled myself.

"Needs must, dear boy. Those men would have taken the artifact, I had to do something."

"You could have thought of something else. What about all those people?" I freed myself from the crazy bugger and stood, brushing myself down. It didn't make any difference, I was still filthy and stinking.

Squinting, I searched the sky for the plane and saw it circling, seemingly under control. It angled down and then disappeared behind the distant view of the city where the airport was. Looked like they'd make it.

"As you can see, they are fine," he said, standing a good distance away from me the other side of the parachute.

"Fine? Fine! You terrified them. There were children on the plane. You should know better, a man of your age."

"Oh," he said with a wry smile, "and what age is that?"

"Huh? Man, you are one freaky-ass dude. I don't know. Sixty-five maybe. Seventy?"

"Arthur, my dear child, you have so much to learn. Do you think I am a simpering fool who knows nothing of this world? I told you I have traveled, that I have seen the world, done things you would not believe. I am an old man, true, but I have many years left yet. Centuries. I am three hundred and forty-seven years old. I have traversed the world thrice over, been married four times, sired countless children, learned magic from many and varied practitioners in numerous countries, and I have been waiting in the desert for this artifact for nigh on fifty years now. I will have it, I will not be denied, and your damn wards will be broken."

"Oh, so you aren't just a nutjob whose become shall we say a tad obsessed with an artifact that could destroy the world?"

"No, I am not," he snapped.

"If you look like one, if you act like one, and if you talk like one..."

"Fool."

"You're an old wizard, so what? And what was with all that locking me up business? You going mad, that was an act?"

"Of course. I thought you would let your guard down, maybe even given in, thinking if you unlocked the box I would let you out and you could take it back, but you are too foolish to take the easy way out, you would rather suffer."

"Trust me, I'd rather not suffer. But no way am I letting you open it, whether you're sane or utterly insane, it makes no difference. You aren't getting it."

I snapped Wand to attention and he shot out a large gobbet of black freaky magic that would have chewed his arm off a little at the wrist but left him mostly okay.

He lifted his hand to protect either the box or his own skin, maybe both. His palm flared white like usual and the assault was easily deflected.

"You are good, but no match for me. Now, if you don't mind, I'll be leaving now."

"You aren't going anywhere, not with that." I pointed at the box in case he didn't know what I was talking about.

"You try and stop me."

So I did.

Decision Time

"This can go one of two ways," he said, standing over me while I rested flat on my back after getting a taster of his magic.

"No third option? I always like a third option as my experience is that the first two always suck."

"No third option, Arthur. You can either release the wards, or you can die here. I'm sorry it has to come to this, I have tried to do the best for you, dear boy, but this has gone on long enough now. Please, Arthur, I'm begging you, let me have it."

"What makes you think you deserve it? You want it, sure, I get that, so does everyone else. But what makes you think you deserve it?"

"Ah, I have pondered that very question on many a night as I sat on my veranda and waited for it to come to me. Here is the truth. I am chosen. I have been patient, knew it was out here in the desert somewhere, and after many a futile search I decided to wait for it to arrive when it was my time. Now is my time. You brought it to me, and that cannot be a coincidence. I deserve it. It is my birthright."

Carefully, I got to my feet, mindful of his power, and faced him. "You got it wrong, whatever your name is. I brought it to you because you have been hanging around wasting your life waiting for it. It doesn't mean you deserve it, it just means you're fool enough to wait longer than anyone else. You're stubborn, and foolish, that doesn't make you special. It makes you like everyone else. You don't know when to call it quits and you refuse to admit there is absolutely no reason why you should have it rather than me or anyone else."

"And couldn't the same be said for you?"

"Yes, of course," I shouted, beyond frustrated, and still shaken by the damn falling from the sky thing. "But there's one big bloody difference. I don't want it, I don't intend to use it, I don't have any plans to ever even touch it. Hell, I don't want to even look at it. What would you do with it anyway?"

"You are a fool. This is what our kind work towards. To be in possession of such an artifact is a true blessing, the pinnacle of our chosen path. We are wizards, this is the ultimate prize."

"Do you know what I do for a living? Or what I did for a living before I had enough money to pick and choose my work?"

"Something untoward I would imagine."

I slumped to the ground, too damn tired to bother standing, too fed up, too pained, too disappointed to bother to be concerned by him. "I steal artifacts. I find out where items are held, and I steal them. I do it for money. I have held, used, found, and sold, countless items of immense power. And all of them were dangerous, but only to a degree. I know artifacts, I know them better than most, maybe even you. And I can tell you this. None of them are to be trusted. Wizards aren't to be trusted, and they made these items, most of them anyway. They are all unstable in ways we only discover when it's too late. This is different. This is the first, the ultimate, the most dangerous, definitely the most volatile, and certainly the most unknown. Nobody knows what it's capable of. Not you, not anyone. And you want to use it? No way."

"As you wish," he said, his head lowering as if he was about to do something unsavory that he'd regret.

"Oh, before you kill me, or try," I said, "you might want to watch out for the falling bits of plane. I nodded at the sky, then smirked.

He frowned, but he looked up nonetheless.

I threw the sand I'd cupped into his face and did the only thing I could think of under the circumstances.

I ran.

Um...

As I stumbled in the desert, tripping on rocks, kicking up sand, and generally making a poor show of scarpering like a proper wizard, I kept expecting him to attack. I'd assumed the next thing I'd see was my brains splattering on the ground in front of me then opening my eyes to be greeted by a very pissed off Death, scythe in hand, foot tapping impatiently.

But no, I kept on running, and nothing happened.

So I ran, and ran some more, because that was all I could think of to do. But then I slowed, and then I stopped, and then I turned around. What was I doing? Why was I running? Ah, yes, he was gonna kill me if I didn't open the box for him. Or was he? Aha, no, he wouldn't, he could have done that already. He was still hoping I'd be of use. Maybe not now, he knew my stance, but maybe in the future if he couldn't get the box open after serious magical interference over the coming months. He wanted me alive as a backup.

I realized just how stupid I'd been. He'd gone. I slapped my forehead for being such a numpty. I couldn't lose him, I might never find him again.

Feeling like a first-class twat, I reluctantly gave chase. Back at the parachute, I scanned the desert. There he was, the sneaky bugger, running hell-for-leather towards the city. A city with countless places to hide and try to disassemble my wards at his leisure. It would take an age to find him, if I ever could, as he could move from place to place and stop me ever getting an exact location.

I picked up the pace, much as my body protested, and ran after an old man headed back into the heart of Dire Dawa.

This was not turning out to be fun, some alone time to put my past behind me. It was the worst damn holiday ever, and I'd had some truly sucky experiences of sand.

Keep Going

The mystery man may have been three hundred and some years older than me, but he was leaving me for dust. To be fair, I wasn't in the best of ways, and I blame the malnutrition, the dehydration, the fighting, the chasing, the falling from planes, but it still rankled as I jogged through the dunes and past the shanty towns, the occasional vehicle and the staring people whilst trying not to collapse.

He was up ahead and in my sights but I couldn't keep up and I certainly couldn't catch him.

Where was he going? What would he do? Would he put others in danger?

With a mighty force of will, and several hurried gulps of water and a mouthful of raisins, which was a bad idea as you try running and swallowing tiny dried grapes without choking, I forced my protesting muscles to obey. Soon the city lay ahead in all its sprawling glory. We chased down roads that morphed from dirt to potholed asphalt, ran past tin-roofed huts and stalls selling fresh fruit and vegetables, dodged goats and scrawny sheep, even several cows or something that looked like them, and then we were on larger roads where the traffic became horrendous.

I'd forgotten in the space of a few weeks just what the city was like. Chaos on an unprecedented scale. Horns blared, people shouted, stalls and stores lined the streets, and wherever we were in the city it was the same old chaos. Everyone seemed to understand how it all worked apart from me. I never could get to grips with the flow of traffic or the fact everyone managed to dodge each other when they all seemed to be moving at random.

It was like a group of ants. If you glanced, there was no rhyme or reason, but if you watched carefully then patterns emerged, order from the chaos. But I was an outsider, wasn't born and bred here, so wasn't privy to how to navigate the madness without getting whacked by planks of wood or being barged into at every turn.

And yet, through it all, I managed to keep him in my sights. He was heading somewhere, and the way he kept glancing over his shoulder meant he was becoming increasingly frustrated with me still following him.

On it went through the afternoon but soon dusk would fall and it would be a different story altogether. There was no way I could keep up the pace, and he knew it. And he knew he just had to give me the slip once and that would be it. Game over for the foreseeable future.

So we continued, me using what little magic I still had available to keep him on my radar. I tapped into the connection we had made, the closeness of weeks, and it allowed me to know more or less where he was whilst he remained near.

We dashed down alleys, we dodged through small markets, we even had a spell in a nice cool, air-conditioned shopping center, and then we were back out into the heat and the blare of the city, through tourist areas and into the true heart of Dire Dawa where it seemed like every other citizen had come to buy supper.

Street vendors and small restaurants all vied for business, shouting out their menus or specials for the day. The smell was intoxicating, utterly bewildering to my senses, and my mouth watered at the thought of sampling the wares. No time, but boy was I tempted.

And then it happened.

I lost him.

The Hunt Is On

So stupid. Why had I run away from him in the first place? Sure, I feared for my life, but I should have thought about it logically. Yeah, tell that to the guy who just jumped from a plane. I regretted it now as I stood amid the hordes all eating street food as the night bore down and the cool air allowed them to enjoy their meals outside surrounded by the hustle and bustle.

He was nowhere to be seen, a ghost. Vanished from right in front of me. He was here a moment ago, where could he be now? I zoned out of the noise, ignored the jostles, the stares, or warnings to get out of the way, and I looked inward, let the connection between magical forces of a very different kind grow stronger.

I felt his presence, and that of the artifact, both linked so tightly now that it was hard to discern one from the other. It didn't matter, as long as they were together then it was all good, or as good as it could currently be.

Letting the magic guide me, I walked without paying attention to my surroundings and followed the trail. He was only minutes ahead of me so I didn't need to panic yet. Not much anyway.

I wandered past smiling men cajoling me to sample mouth-watering barbecue. I ignored women adorned with gold hoops up their arms and brightly colored headdresses who sweetly promised I was in for a treat if I stepped inside and ordered the curry, and I refused to be suckered into buying jewelry from men with crooked teeth and even more crooked hearts.

What I did was follow a shadow through the streets and alleys that were out-of-bounds to those who didn't belong. I got stares from hard men standing in the shadows of doorways protecting whatever nefarious things went on inside. I got warned off by groups of skinny youths in ragged t-shirts and tattered shorts who stood around guardedly dealing whatever the latest drug was that had taken hold and ruined a new wave of lives. I moved past them all, paid them no mind, and they knew they could only push so far before they looked away and resumed their business.

Why had he chosen this part of the city? If I looked foreign then he looked positively alien here. He didn't have the swagger, didn't have the look to have a hope of getting through here without some serious trouble. Unless they knew him, or knew of him. Or maybe his very oddness would work in his favor. The fact he was so out-of-place could go in his favor if he could act nonchalant enough. He clearly wasn't a tourist, had the African way about him in many regards, but he was also typically British.

And yet he continued to move, always several steps ahead, and as the night wore on and we wormed our way through the heart of darkness, I knew he was heading somewhere specific rather than merely trying to throw me off the scent by haunting the unsavory parts of a mostly beautiful, rich, and vibrant city.

I was seriously flagging by now though, and I knew myself well enough to know that soon I would be unable to continue. As I turned down one dark alley then the next, waded through filth and skipped over small streams running between houses clogged with detritus and stinking to high heaven, I was just about out of steam.

My foot caught on the cracked road and I stumbled, unable to halt my fall. My hands made contact with a damp squelch as they sank into a mire of rotten garbage. Well, it probably wouldn't make me smell any worse, which was about all I could say that wouldn't be censored as I clambered shakily to my feet. I shook off the worst of it, the sticky coating refusing to budge even after wiping my hands on my combats, so I staggered on into the night, following a fading scent of magic and misfortune, pining for my old life where I had clean tea towels and coffee any time I wanted it.

Such luxuries gnawed at me as I waded, filthy and weak, through streets full of those in similar dire circumstances. We were more alike now, one and the same. Undernourished, overworked, unsure of the future. Except, my misery was temporary, I hadn't lived my whole life like this.

This isn't to say that this city was different to others, they were all the same once you cut through the thin veneer of respectability and surface shine. The richest cities on the planet had their fair share of poverty, and the more wealth that flowed through them the harder those at the bottom had it. Here, people smiled at you who in other countries would offer nothing but a frown or tears. It could make you forget their plight, how hard they had it, but the back streets were different.

Away from the lights and the commerce, were those who lived a different life. A criminal life often forced upon them out of necessity, sometimes chosen as an easy way out rather than the only way out. Those were the ones you had to watch out for, the individuals who enjoyed the fear they instilled, the death they caused, the heartache they forced upon defenseless families on a nightly basis.

This was where I was at, and I did not like it one bit. It was too familiar, too close for comfort, as this was where I had spent much of my life. Mixing with the scum, the desperate, the cruel, and the merciless.

I was all of those things too, and worse, but I tried not to be, even though I failed. What I wanted was to be a good guy but good guys are boring and turn their backs on opportunities to have fun and go on adventures, and if there was one thing I always was, it's adventurous. Although I'd rather have them in my own country so I didn't have to travel far.

Foul of body, clothes, and heart, I put my gangster walk into full effect, dared anyone to say a cross word to me or even look at me funny. Shadowy figures receded into the doorways, kids scrambled for cover, and even the rats ran away as The Hat passed. He was seriously pissed now, and they knew it.

An old hand at playing the hard man, I kept my muscles relaxed, my neck loose, and scanned the area ahead without making eye contact with anyone for more than the briefest moment. They saw I meant business, was a man of the streets, and they left me alone with my demons.

Into the Night

There was no use denying it any longer. I'd lost him. He was close, annoyingly so, but every time I felt his presence, knew in my bones he was just around another corner, that all I had to do was speed up and take a turn, he was gone by the time I dragged my sorry arse there.

The bond between him and the artifact was strong, stronger than ever, or maybe I was merely getting better at tuning in to them both. I felt the artifact, felt my wards struggling against his constant barrage, and I felt him, his desperation, his frustration, and his fear.

For he was scared. Of me, of the artifact, of what it could do, even of the depraved parts of the city he'd entered, but what he was most terrified of was losing it all. Of me snatching the artifact from him and him never getting a second chance. He knew this was his one shot. Lose it, and there would be no replay.

So he moved fast and silent through the city, took twists and turns he knew well, better than me, and never once stopped for more than a few moments. My guess was it had been some time since he'd familiarized himself with the back alleys, and not everything in such a city is static. Buildings come and go, alleys get blocked up, others become too dangerous even for him, and yet he always found a way to keep moving, to never let me catch him.

And I knew I couldn't. That the best I could hope for was to keep giving chase and never give him the chance to rest. Keep on going, always one step behind, and offer no respite. Eventually he'd have to stop, he'd simply have to, but this game could not continue. I didn't have it in me, not any more. I was empty of everything but grim determination, but my resolve wasn't enough to allow me to hunt until my prey was captured and the infernal prize was mine.

I tripped yet again in more rotten filth, then used a crumbling wall for support to right myself. As I staggered on, I came to a halt at a corner and peered around into yet another poorly lit street. He was gone again, and so it would continue.

No more, I could not do this for another minute.

I shook and I shivered and I almost collapsed right there and then, but this was no place to leave yourself exposed to the desperate and the despicable. Taking a moment to gain a sense of place within this vast crush of humanity, I did some dubious mental arithmetic then turned around and headed off, leaving him to his desperate wandering. I then realized he wouldn't know if I was following him or not, didn't have the connection I had, so my only hope was that he would tire himself out while I rested up a while.

Several shaky minutes later, I was back in the hubbub of the beautiful city where people gossiped and shouted, smiled and laughed, slapped each other on the back and settled down for drinks or dinner. Lights shone bright from stalls and stores and I have never been so pleased to be accosted by people desperate to sell me live chickens, which had happened more often than you'd think.

Mindful of the state I was in, and amazed anyone came anywhere near me, I sought out one of the wash houses that littered such areas. These shanty towns had dubious water supplies and amenities and much washing and laundry was a communal affair. I found a typical place soon enough.

A large open space surrounded by towering buildings of brick, block, and corrugated iron, there were numerous raised platforms with large pools of water for the washing of clothes. Hoses snaked across the cracked concrete. Freezing, and shivering, I nonetheless stripped and hosed myself and my clothes down before going to a laundry platform. I gave my clothes a good scrub, and me along with it, used handfuls of scooped-up soap pieces that littered the area. It was far from perfect, it was far from enjoyable, but who was I to complain?

This was as good as it got for many, and lots even appreciate it. Those who came in from the desert found water on demand like this almost miraculous, so washed their clothes without grumble whereas I complained if the washing machine back at home took too long and moaned about the price of detergent.

Clean, or cleanish, but freezing and naked, I hung my clothes on a line and checked nobody was around. Before I collapsed, I used what fragments of diffuse magic still resided inside me and I let a warm wind blow against my clothes, drying the worst of the cold off them and then, unable to control the elements for a moment more, I numbly dressed in damp gear that was at last semi-clean and felt a hell of a lot better for it.

Right, what was next?

I left the wash area, found the nearest stall selling warm food, and slumped into a rickety metal chair at a table. I pulled out cash, handed it to the grinning stall holder, and told her to keep feeding me until my money ran out. She said it would be a long night with that much money and I said that was fine, and so she began to serve me in a very timely fashion.

As the night wore on and people came and went, so my energy levels rose. Between plates of warm goat, rice, hot drinks of goats milk laden with sugar, and repeats of the limited menu, I dozed, each mini sleep longer than the last until I found myself being shaken by the smiling, if now somewhat concerned woman, telling me it was time for her to leave, that she appreciated the money but it was almost dawn and she had to go home to see to her children.

I thanked her for her help, and then she was gone, pushing her cart away into a sleeping city.

Almost sleeping, The Hat stirred. He was fed and watered, had even shucked off the worst of his weariness, and so was ready for battle to commence once more.

Getting Ready

As I straightened in my chair, my body creaking and groaning more than usual, I planned what to do next. What I was sorely tempted to do was find the hotel and go rest up for a few days so I was fully fighting fit, but I knew it would take weeks or months to recover properly from all my wounds, both physical and mental, and I wasn't sure I could bear to be inside a room of any sort after my incarceration.

Plus, I knew if I went back there, had a big hug from Sameena, and enjoyed her food and company, I would become sidetracked, lose my edge. No, I had to continue to suffer, to feel like shit, and be miserable. It would give me the edge I needed to capture him, and I knew I'd need every ounce of dogged determination I could muster if I was to pull this off.

But I really wanted to go home, ached for my old life, and although I knew deep down I wouldn't, couldn't do it, I was sorely tempted to leave him and the artifact here, forget the whole sorry affair. It wasn't an option though, not if I had an ounce of humanity, and I did, more's the pity.

So I got myself together, was surprised to discover my backpack on a chair next to me and not stolen, and I hoisted it onto my shoulders, lifted my face to the sun as it rose over the skyscrapers of Dire Dawa, and turned slowly in a circle until I felt the drag of wards lead me into the heart of the city once more.

My idea of rest and a little recuperation was misguided. I'd thought it would help me find the thief easier, allow me to move faster through the city and catch him once I had his location pinpointed. What I hadn't banked on was being unable to find him in the first place. I sensed the wards, had a feeling for the artifact and him, but it wasn't like the day before. That deep connection was lost. All I had was a trace, like a fleeting breeze, hinting at their whereabouts.

Instead of having a map in my head, I had something more akin to an inkling of a feeling of a suggestion of them maybe being somewhere nearby as I scoured the city by foot, not risking transport for fear of ending up gridlocked or going in completely the wrong direction.

I wandered, had to stop repeatedly to fine-tune my senses; frustration grew as I got no closer to putting an end to this. Several times I thought I had him, or was close, only to find I was wrong, had picked up on nefarious magic or wards guarding other artifacts I currently had no interest in but at other times would have been itching to take for myself.

On and on it went throughout the day. The heat of the city was stifling and claustrophobic. Countless thousands of people rammed into the city made it unbearable, yet bear it I did, along with the rest of them. My sweat-stained clothes that stuck to ravaged flesh were covered in dust and grime, and it became increasingly difficult to breathe as I moved through heavily congested traffic that blocked the roads at every turn.

By late afternoon I was dashing about like the demented Englishmen I surely was, causing quite a stir as locals watched me hurry this way and that, repeatedly passing them as they sat in the shade watching the world go by or languidly got about their own business, still amazed I was out in heat they knew you should never rush through.

I was going round and a round in circles, no closer to catching him. What was I thinking? Why had I stopped yesterday? I should have kept going until I couldn't move another step. Haha, that's exactly what I had done, and that hadn't worked. No, I'd made the right call, and I would catch him. He would not escape me, he couldn't, it didn't bear thinking about.

And so it continued. Me getting closer, narrowing down the search as he kept on the move, still not risking holing up somewhere. Maybe he'd rested during the night same as me. Maybe he could sense if I was close, he was certainly powerful enough if he was focused, so he would be rested of a sorts and able to carry this on until I gave up or he succumbed to true madness, which he would eventually.

Then, just like that, even though the day had been never-ending and had sapped what little energy I'd regained, darkness fell like a hammer on the city and once more everything changed.

Criminals emerged from their lairs. Pickpockets, chancers, gangs, lone assassins, the desperate, the needy, the homeless, all of them woke as the sun set. But that wasn't the whole story. Along with the troublesome came the hard workers, those looking for cheap food, and company. People who had worked hard all day and wanted to enjoy the cool evening of the city. It became vibrant in a different way, but there was an edge to the atmosphere in the places I moved through, and I kept wondering why he had chosen the rougher side of town rather than somewhere more suited to his needs and preferences.

It was obvious he liked his comforts even though he'd lived in the desert. He had a nice home with plenty of convenience, this was the last place you'd expect to find him. Maybe he thought it would throw me off, maybe he liked it, maybe he knew it better, or maybe he figured he could hide easier. I assumed the latter. Of course, he was right. It may have been dangerous to some, but it was one hell of a place to hide.

I searched, I got no closer. He was good, and he was bloody annoying.

"That's it," I said as I stopped in my tracks. "If you want to play hard to get then it's time I upped my game."

With a dramatic swish of my jacket, which didn't quite work as it wasn't long enough or swishy enough, I spun on my heels and went to pay a group of "people" a visit much as I was loathe to do so. Desperate times call for desperate measures, and boy was I desperate.

Drama Much?

Africa as a whole, maybe Ethiopia in particular, is a place of vast contradictions. Modern yet steeped in history, forthright yet shy, striving to become first world, yet unable to pull away from third world poverty. Rich yet incredibly poor, Christian yet entrenched in much more ancient religions, traditional and yet many people strove to pull away from the old ways and become part of the new. And definitely brimming with magic.

People here believe. Not just willing to consider the presence of magic, they embrace it, accept it, know it exists. From witch doctors who ran the villages, wise elders, witches, and spell casters, the history of magic use here goes back to the beginning. Everyone knows it is a real thing, everyone understands there are those who can contact the dead, that spirits and ghosts, demons and angels, are real entities, that other dimensions exist, and there are things we cannot see let alone understand. It is accepted as part of being human, that there is more to the world than we could possibly know, and everyone in their right mind is scared of such things.

Which is why cemeteries here are such strange places. The dead are venerated, sometimes even worshiped, and graves are either well-tended with flowers and beads, trinkets and candles lit regularly, or nobody goes near them for fear of having their souls taken.

At my wits' end, I had come to visit one such cemetery, a place full of spirits and the dead refusing to rest. Haunted, and overflowing with magic because people believed and thus their belief was manifest.

This was no modern cemetery, no traditional resting place as we in the west think of one. The sacred ground was old, older than the city as it now stood, older than many countries. This was a place where the land was so ancient, the bodies buried so long ago, that they were laid to rest on top of each other. Graves dug on the old ones covered by sand over the centuries until the original inhabitants were so deep they couldn't claw their way out no matter how much their ancestors wished them to be re-animated.

There was also the ongoing problem of disinterment, which was why so many graves were deeper than usual and why so many people buried their relatives not in ordinary plots but in small rooms with locked metal doors or had the entrance bricked up entirely. Those who embraced the dark arts of re-animation loved nothing more than an unattended grave of the recently deceased to practice their craft on. It wasn't as much of a problem as in the old days, but it still happened on occasion. What was more likely these days was for the spirit to be contacted by distraught relatives, often coming to the place of their burial.

The tombs, the mausoleums, and the stone coffins with slabs of rock for lids were so old and weather-worn many looked like they had been carved from single pieces of rock, the joins and the inscriptions long gone, filled by sand compressed through the ages until it was hard to tell what was a natural rock and what was man-made. Built in an unusual spot on the outskirts of the city, the whole area was stepped with large rocky outcrops perfect for sitting and surveying the strange place.

I sat on one such large flat expanse at the top of a series of winding steps carved directly into the rock and dangled my feet over the edge thirty feet above the ground.

In many ways it was a beautiful sight, the worn stones, the headstones, the many and varied mausoleums that housed the dead and the not-so-dead. Plastic flowers caught the light from candles and the more modern lights strung along wires laced haphazardly throughout the whole area. It was peaceful after the chaos of the city but not as silent as you would imagine, especially for a wizard attuned to the cries of the tormented. Those who either refused to accept their fate or who preferred to hang around their final resting place, unwilling or unable to pass on for one reason or another. The people buried here had believed in the spirit world, so were more capable of resisting the lure of the afterlife and embracing the next stage.

They understood it and thus could choose more readily what their fate would be. It was never a good choice. Once you're dead you should move on, but they made the decision so had to endure the consequences.

I shut my ears to their cries, their moans, their wailing, their lamenting, and steeled myself for what I was about to do.

Was it a good idea? No, probably not. Did I have any other ones? Absolutely not.

With a sigh, I got to my feet and went to call on some old acquaintances. They were still here, I knew that. What better place than this for those who didn't fear death like mere mortals? Plus, there was always somewhere suitably spooky to rest during the day, and they did enjoy the drama.

Second Thoughts

"What am I doing?" I muttered as I stood outside the crumbling mausoleum with my hand raised to the rusty iron gates.

I shook my head to dispel the doubts; I'd already changed my mind a handful of times and now wasn't the time to change it again. Did I have a choice? Of course. Did I have a better plan? No. Would this work? Probably not. Was there a chance it would? Yes. Should I go get a coffee first? Undoubtedly.

Without further ado, I turned the handle on the utterly oversized and ridiculously spooky gate and pushed inward. It opened with a blood-curdling creak that rose in pitch as the hinges swung the heavy gate inward. They actually worked on the hinges to make them like this, all part of the drama.

Inside was pitch black, no light entered from outside, as if too afraid of what it might find, and I didn't blame it. The entrance had no locks for one simple reason. Nobody would dare disturb the occupants unless they had an excellent reason, because if they didn't, it would be the last thing they ever did.

The door banged open against the stone wall and a dull thud echoed around the chamber before it was sucked up by the vastness. The air was cool in here, and the thick stone walls kept the temperature relatively constant, just how the occupants liked it. I'm not afraid to admit that I was close to freaking out a little, even though such dramatics weren't anything new. But it wasn't the spooky effects or the place itself that bothered me, it was what was inside, or more correctly, who was inside.

There are vampires, and there are Vampires. There are those back home and those who are things apart, of a very different breed. Sure, we get the spooky ones in the UK too, all countries have them. Those who live as close to the old ways as possible, who embrace what they are and have no interest in blending in with society, hiding in plain sight. Who grow their nails long, their hair likewise, and remain aloof and apart from citizens, mixing only with their own. But even those types are modern in many ways, liked comfort and money, dress normally when out and about, venture into the world of man and appear mostly normal, if a little odd.

And then there are true vampires, old skool to the max, who are nothing like the humans they once were. Vampires in every regard, utterly unlike any you are likely to meet. Why? Because chances are very high that if you ever meet one of these guys it would be curtains for you.

These were traditionalists in every regard. Had no interest in money, houses, cars, jewelry, kitchen gadgets, even a nice coffee machine. Never wore modern clothes, never cared what others thought, and never, ever mixed with humans. They thought of us as little but food, fodder for their powers, and so far beneath them we were hardly even thought about. To them we were animals that occupied the same planet but little more. We were there for them, to feed them, and what we got up to, human politics, the rat race, the jobs, the striving to make things better, any of it, they simply did not care one iota. We were an infestation, and they paid us absolutely no mind.

And I'd come to ask them a favor.

I stepped inside. The gate clanged shut behind me.

Waking the Beasties

It seemed like a good idea to have light, so I pulled a sleepy Wand out and shook him to life. He wasn't happy about it, grumbled semi-coherently about him being magical wood from the land of the fae, not a bloody torch, and blah, blah, blah, but he brightened the room with a cool orange glow that cast deep shadows and did nothing to improve the ambience. I'm sure he did it on purpose. If he wanted, he could have lit it up like daytime, but I wasn't about to get into an argument in the middle of a vampire den about light quality. Plus, they might have objected if it was too bright. They did like to keep it dark in these here parts.

I moved slowly, trying my best not to appear threatening, which wasn't difficult. I was in a single large space with flagstone floors and stone walls, stone roof, and stone sarcophagi. Large ones, with lids no human could hope to move, made from single slices of thick rock in daily use for centuries if not millennia. But they no longer housed the original occupants, they'd been evicted long ago. Now they had new owners, and they weren't dead, not really, although maybe a bit. It's always hard to tell with vampires just what the deal is and if they're even alive in the traditional sense at all.

Whatever, they were here, they were resting, but soon they would awake and I didn't want to make our first meeting in decades begin on the wrong foot.

As true night fell, so they began to slowly stir. Old vampires go into a deep rest akin to hibernation, slow down until they are almost dead. They take a while to come out of their slumber, for their bodies to get up to speed, and the ones I was visiting were mostly very old, with a few newcomers thrown in to keep things interesting and the gang with sufficient numbers. But there was a hierarchy, and the younger ones, those turned in the last century or so, the babes, knew better than to get out of their beds before the old dudes. It was just good manners.

Noise filled the musty room. Raspy breathing, clawing at stone, that kind of thing. Either they knew they had company, or they were amusing themselves and gearing up for a night of fun.

I moved to the middle of the room, stepped cautiously around the large coffins until I was standing next to the largest, simplest, and oldest of them all. The massive lid shifted, grinding stone against stone, and I took several steps back to allow the sleepy vampire some space to move.

The lid slid sideways until half the interior was exposed and a black, clawed hand gripped tight to the side. A torso slowly sat upright, naked, well-muscled, skin smooth yet covered in dust sticking to streaks of dried blood and who knew what else. He was filthy, made me seem like Mr. Fresh and Sparkly, but this was their way. They reveled in their base nature, got all kinds of crazed when they fed, and loved the scent of their victims on their skin.

The vampire's head turned to face me, a handsome face in many ways, but the eyes stopped him being attractive. They were cold, and pale, and icy blue. He looked at me like I was dirt under his feet, of no importance and less interest. The look of a predator. Wand's orange glow bounced off his bald head, reminding me of a bowling ball. I held my mirth at bay; he probably wouldn't see the funny side if I mentioned it.

"Arthur," he hissed, the single word conveying so much about him. That he was truly African, but had traveled and knew many languages, that he found me tiresome, that he thought nothing of me, and that he was my superior.

"Otangu," I acknowledged with a nod of the head.

"You have returned."

"Looks that way. Not for long, hopefully." I offered my hand and he took it with a slight incline of his head, as if it was expected and I should be pleased to serve him. He gripped firmly, but not unkindly so, and I helped him out of his bed.

Otangu stretched his arms overhead and yawned; his teeth snicked down as he did so. "Hungry," he said, as he turned to stare at me with a wide smile.

"Yeah, I bet. Have you grown? You look like you have."

"Haha, always the funny man. No, merely still taller than you puny humans."

Otangu, like the others in his intimate tribe, was tall by any standards. Seven feet at least, but in proportion, and quite buff with it. His diet obviously agreed with him. If his gang ever decided to take up basketball they'd be winners for sure.

"So, what's new?" I asked as other lids were scraped aside and his posse emerged. In the blink of an eye, I was surrounded by giant, dark-skinned vampires eyeing me greedily, craning forward on strong necks to sniff me and lick their lips. I really wished I was at home snuggling up to Penelope, that would have been much nicer times a billion.

"We feed, we play, we revel in the gift we have been bestowed. We are the true ones, we flourish. Our numbers grow and the humans run in fear. Life is good, Arthur Salzman, same as always." Otangu put an arm around a naked female vampire with huge pendulous breasts and fondled her gently. She purred at his touch, her head flung back, then when he stopped she turned on me and hissed.

I jumped. They laughed. Vampires and their games, never ceases to be hysterical.

"You busy?" I asked, not wanting to push things but wanting to get going on what I had planned.

"I would rather do anything than help you, Arthur, but if I must," he said with a sigh, knowing as well as I did that he had no choice. It still meant I had to tread carefully, he wasn't to be trusted, but he was in my debt and that debt had to be paid if I asked.

"Hey, no pressure," I said, holding my hands out. "It's up to you. I have a favor to ask, is all. If you don't want to do it then fine. Just thought I'd ask." This was all part of the game, to make it seem like I wasn't bothered, that I didn't have a hold over him, so he could reluctantly agree to help without losing face or it appearing like I was telling him what to do. Because, whether he owed me one or not, if I made him lose face he would rip my throat out and live with the broken favor he was duty-bound to repay.

It was all about tradition, about repaying your debt to someone, and he owed me big time. He knew it, I knew it, they all knew it, but that didn't matter as much as maintaining the facade of superiority, that he was royalty and I was the peasant who should prostrate himself before the king and be thankful he was in his presence at all.

It went against everything I believed in, for normally I would bow to no man, and wouldn't even to him, but this was how the game was played and I wanted his help so what was a poor wizard to do?

"I may have a little time to help you if you would like?" he said, not sounding like he was too keen.

"That would be most kind. Hopefully it won't take long, and it would mean a lot. I know it's beneath you, such a paltry thing to ask, but I'm sure if you did this thing then we would be free of any further obligations to one another."

"Obligation?" he growled, getting right up in my face, the stench of death all around him.

"Um, not obligation, assistance. We would not need to assist each other ever again."

"Haha, you should have seen your face. So funny." Otangu laughed loudly and the others joined in.

Vampires sure are a funny lot. Not.

The Gang's All Here

"We will do this favor for you," said Otangu, "and then I do not expect to see you again."

"What, and miss out on my charming wit?"

"Do not try my patience, pesky human. You forget with whom you speak."

I knew damn well with whom I spoke. A murderous vampire with no morals. An animal who owed me a favor and now I was here to collect. He could dick about all he wanted, he owed me and he had no choice. I'd still expected more messing about than this though. For him to try to weasel out of it somehow. Guess I'd forgotten quite how highly he regarded duty and honor.

"So you'll do it?"

"I will. Let us go and be done with this."

The entire group moved towards the entrance with a nod from Otangu.

"Wait, don't you want to know what you'll be doing first?"

"Whatever it is, it shall be done. You may ask us outside. I miss the night, the cold, the emptiness. We will go, then you may speak."

Damn but I hated these traditionalists. They were no fun.

Outside, they amassed on the large slab I'd recently been sitting on. They were there in a heartbeat, I had to walk up the steps like a normal person.

Otangu stood with his back to the precipice, his feet balanced right on the edge. His followers gathered around him. He beckoned me with a crook of a finger so I joined him, somewhat reluctantly, and not quite so close to the edge.

"Tell us," he ordered.

"Okay, there's this man, an old man who lived in the desert. Been there for fifty years or so."

"The wizard," said one of the women.

"Yeah, a wizard. Old guy, lived there alone, had a nice house. I've, er, been visiting my old master, and then went for a walk, and I came across him. He stole something from me, it's in a wooden box, and he has it. He's in the city, I can't catch him, so I'd be grateful if you could get him for me."

"We shall find him and we shall each taste his blood. You may have your box and then you may leave."

"Wait! Whoa there. No killing. Just the box, and what's inside, that's all I want." Otangu and the others scowled at me like I'd lost my mind. "What?"

"This man stole what is yours but you do not want him dead? You are a strange wizard."

"Yeah, I know, it's the British way. Please, just the box."

"As you wish. We will merely take a taste, not kill him. Have a little fun then return what you have lost."

"No, you don't get it. Don't hurt him, he's harmless. Well, sort of. Just the box."

"You dare tell me what to do?" barked Otangu, all pleasantries gone. Damn, he was still as touchy as always.

I sighed. "I wasn't telling you, I was asking, but can we please cut the bullshit? You owe me, and big time. All this fucking dancing around the subject, you acting the big man, spare me the crap. You are in my debt, and I'm here to collect."

I think I may have gone a bit too far. Nobody said a word, nobody moved. I held my breath and waited for a group of seven-feet-tall vampires to devour me, and not in a nice way.

Otangu laughed and placed an arm around my shoulder. Luckily, he didn't fondle me.

"Haha, you are a brave man, my friend. Come, let us do this thing for you and then we shall be even. I like you, Arthur, always have. So different to the other humans. So direct, unafraid, a true brave spirit. You are almost vampire."

"Gee, thanks for the compliment. So, we good?"

"Oh yes, my friend, we are very good indeed. Now, please tell me all about this man and where we are likely to find him."

The mood relaxed, which wasn't hard as it had been positively icy, and I told them all about the mystery man and how I'd been chasing him and where he was at the moment, at least best I could tell. Whilst I spoke, the vamps limbered up, stretched their frames out, cricked bones, yawned with boredom, then became increasingly edgy as they wanted to get going. Probably wanted a quick feed on the way.

What Otangu didn't ask was what was in the box. He didn't care, had no interest in artifacts or money or anything of that nature. All they needed was each other's company, food, and a nice slab to rest under during the day.

With a word from Otangu, his clan were gone, off at vampire top speed to scour the city and bring the thief back to the cemetery.

Once we were alone, Otangu squatted on his haunches and looked up at me. "This will be the end of it," he warned. "I will have repaid my debt and we will owe each other nothing. How I regret you helping me, how I have cursed your name, waiting for you to return. I do not like being in your debt, wizard, it is not our way. You will not come back, or I will destroy you."

"Sure thing. I never planned to return, never planned to call in the favor. But this is important, and I would never have asked otherwise."

"You would have left the debt unpaid? You would not have wanted the favor returned?" he asked, shocked.

"That's right. I didn't help you to be owed one, I helped because it saved lives."

"So strange, you humans. I will never understand you."

"And yet you were one, once upon a time."

"Please, do not remind me. But that was not the man you see before you. That was a different person, a weaker one, and it was so very long ago. People change."

"They sure do."

With that, he was gone. I stood alone and listened to the wails of the deceased.

Memories

When I was here last time, amongst other things I had an encounter with a vampire. Make that several. I was in the desert, had been for a while, and in dire shape. But not as dire as Otangu and his cohorts. They were the adventurous type even back then, and loved nothing more than to hunt. Bored with the city and the easy pickings, they'd decided to have a short vacation out in the wilds, getting back to basics kind of thing, even though they lived about as basically as you could get already.

That right there was a huge mistake. The one thing they'd overlooked was that the desert was just that. Deserted. They'd chased down a couple of tourists and gone to town on them over several days, catching them, having a taste, then releasing them only to give them a head start before resuming the fun and games. Otangu told me all this with relish when I met him and his cronies, as if I'd be impressed. I wasn't.

They'd eventually put the poor young couple out of their misery and when I came across them it was to find his group sitting amongst the remains, nothing left but bone and two ransacked backpacks. Otangu and his people were in a terrible state. They'd chased the couple too far out into the desert and had made the fatal mistake of hunting until the early morning, caught up in the excitement as they were, and were now fretting about what would happen when the sun rose.

I found them wailing, curled up tight in balls, weak as kittens, intermittently catching fire before dousing each other only to heal and for the cycle to be repeated over and over.

I stood there watching for some time, the scene before me obvious. I wouldn't save them, had no interest in doing so, for I knew the type and I knew what they had done, if not the gruesome details.

Otangu had asked me for help, ordered me in fact, but I shook my head and told them if they were stupid enough to get caught out like this then that was their own damn fault. He swore at me and said it was unfortunate but that they would survive, that they always did, and had built up enough immunity to overcome the sun although it would leave them weak for a while. I thought it was bravado, but couldn't be sure. He spoke with dignity and grace even as he burned, and then he proceeded to tell me what they had done, how it had happened.

My mind was firmly made up then. No assistance from the tired, sunburned wizard.

It was at this point that my friend Marcus made an appearance, along with his tribe. I spied them off in the distance the same as Otangu, and knew the vampires would be on them if I didn't do something. What followed was a hasty bargain made between us. I told him I would help them if they promised to leave the nomads alone. He agreed.

I headed off to the nomads and told them of my finding in the desert and they promised to change course so they'd avoid the vamps. You'd think they would be shocked by my tale, that I would be laughed at as a crazy foreigner who'd been out in the sun too long, but this was the desert, and people here believed. They gave me poles, and light canvas, and I promised I would return soon.

With the vampires laid out under the shade, they quickly regained their composure and the group began to plot their next meal. Otangu silenced them with a sharp warning, that they had made a deal and it was not to be broken under any circumstances. He had honor, and his word was good, and they had better act the same upon pain of death.

I was surprised by his outburst, by his insistence on being true to his word, and so they went hungry, slept through the day, and when night came they left to return with all haste to the city.

Before they went, Otangu told me he was in my debt, and it was clear he didn't like it. And that was that, apart from when I got back to the city and I checked them out, paid a brief visit during the day to see where they lived, beating a hasty retreat before they woke.

It was so long ago, and I still wasn't sure if I'd done the right thing or not, as how many lives had been taken since? But after meeting Marcus I was glad I'd saved him, let him have a beautiful life. Such is the way of things, never clear cut, never sure if what you do is right or terribly wrong.

But I knew when I saved the vampires that it was worth the risk, because even if I hadn't they would probably have survived, even if left in a bad way, and then they would have continued their murder spree, killed the nomads, hunted me down, and no lives at all would have been spared.

That's what I told myself at night when memories kept me from the mini-death I so often craved.

My thoughts were disturbed by the sound of crying. I watched a lone woman bend to a new grave and lay flowers. She looked exhausted, and sad beyond belief, probably at work until this ungodly hour then come to pay respects to her loved one.

Sometimes life is so fucking sad. I wanted to console her, but it wouldn't take away her pain, would only add to mine, so I turned my back to her and sat on the rock listening to a woman cry over the hurt we all suffer. She stopped eventually, left to return home, and then it was just me and the lost souls.

Guess I was a lost soul too. I thought I'd been found, had gained peace, but being here made me realize I was as lost as I'd ever been, maybe more so.

Old Acquaintances

"The debt is repaid in full," said Otangu as the entire group appeared beside me.

"Bloody hell, whistle or something so I know you're coming." I got myself together and reluctantly moved from where I'd been lying on my back, contemplating life's many injustices.

"We are vampires, we do not whistle. The debt is paid. Now, be gone." Otangu pushed a freaked-out old man clutching a box towards me but he came up short when he reached the end of his tether. A thin rope tied around his neck that tightened as he strained against it.

"Thanks, but was that necessary?"

"He tried to use his magic on us. On us! He is lucky to be alive. Take him, and go. I do not wish to see you again, wizard." Otangu passed over the rope to me and the vampires parted. We were free to leave.

I nodded to him, then spoke to the old man. "Time to go, and time to hand over what's mine."

"Enough chatter. You are trespassing. Leave, and fast."

"Hand it over," I hissed, but the stubborn mule clutched the box tighter and held his head up to meet my gaze.

"Never."

"Goddammit!" I yanked on the rope and strode past the vampires before Otangu decided to have a tasty double wizard snack now his debt of honor was repaid in full. I led the thief away and didn't turn around or even run, much as I wanted to do both.

We left the cemetery, me pulling the rope taut, infusing it with what magic I had as we went so he couldn't just burn through it and escape. I knew it wouldn't last long, that this was temporary at best, but I only needed it to hold for a few minutes and then this would all be over.

"Don't try anything," I warned. "I've had a crap night and the last few weeks have been even worse, so I'm in no mood for your nonsense."

"You cannot hold me, I am more than your equal," he said, but he sounded resigned, and we both knew I had the upper hand for now.

"One more word out of you and I'll give you to the vampires. All it takes is one shout out and you're food for the blood suckers."

"I heard what Otangu said. He owes you no favors."

"You think eating you would be a favor? Ha, he'll kill you because that's what he does, not because I want him too."

"And then he'll eat you too."

The sneaky bugger had a point, but I said nothing and dragged him around the corner into a nice dark alley so we could finish our business.

We faced each other, me with the rope tight, half the length wrapped around my hand. "If you make a move, try anything, then I will yank this rope as hard as I can and you'll get your scrawny neck broken. Understand?" He nodded. "Good. Now, slowly, bend down and place the box on the ground."

"No. Never."

What was with him? Didn't he know when he'd been beaten?

Reluctantly, I tensed my muscles then yanked as hard as I could on the rope.

His neck snapped and he crumpled to the ground. Yay me.

I felt bloody awful. What was it about this man that had got to me so? He'd stolen, locked me up, starved me, almost killed me, tried to kill me in fact, and yet for some reason I was sad to see him go.

I reached down to retrieve the box and was flung back against the wall, smacked my head hard, then blacked out.

Ugh

When I came to a moment later, it was to find myself alone in the alley. The old guy was gone, the box was gone, even the rope was gone.

Wasn't this bloody typical. I had him, I killed him, I lost him. And I lost the artifact. Again.

Rather than waste energy and be annoyed standing up, I remained seated and got angry whilst also conserving energy. My head throbbed, the lump was large, but my thick skull didn't appear to be cracked so that was excellent news.

I replayed the final scene in my mind, wondering what had happened. I saw him refuse to release the box, saw his eyes widen as he realized I wasn't messing about and tugged the rope hard. I saw the power run down the rope, saw it snap hard and impossibly tight around his neck, and heard his neck break and saw him fall, dead, to the ground.

Then what?

I bent to retrieve the box and was sent flying.

How?

I hit mental rewind and slowed things down, went over it once more. What happened as I bent to get the artifact? Where did the assault come from? The box? His body? Was it his death curse? Nope, not that, sure didn't feel like it. What then?

There was only one answer to such a puzzle. He wasn't dead. I went over it again. Ah, yes, there it was. Just as I was about to get my hands on the box a powerful streak of energy burst from his outstretched hand, a hand that was conveniently pointed right at me. Then I was sailing away to have a meeting with a wall.

He wasn't dead, that was the obvious answer so must be true. But I'd broken his neck, hadn't I? Yes, I had. So he was seriously injured. You couldn't survive that though, could you? Guess you could.

Wizards are funny creatures. We can get up to all sorts, and if we have a mind, we can put up with a lot of discomfort, even injuries that should kill us. He was old, strong, and damn stubborn, so if he had enough strength, enough power inside, he could have channeled it just in time to stop himself dying from such an injury. It would have been a close call, and hurt like hell, but magic is mysterious, and works in all kinds of ways, so I should have known he'd pull something like that.

One thing was for sure, he wouldn't be fighting fit now, far from it. His damn neck was still broken, his power was all used up, and he would need a lot of rest to heal from such a serious injury.

Time was of the essence so I better get my skates on. I heaved up from the wall and limped out of the alley.

Damn Annoyed

Night was upon us, true night. When hard workers were laying exhausted in their beds having nightmares about the day to come. When most people were safe behind locked doors and only the insomniacs, the thrill-seekers, the night workers, or the stupid were out and about. Guess I was one of the latter.

Cursing myself for losing him after being handed him on a plate, I focused, refused to be distracted, and promised myself that next time I saw this utterly annoying old man I would kill him instantly and be done with his crap for good.

I just had to find him first.

How far could you get when your neck was broken and you looked like a low-budget zombie?

Quite far it turned out, as no matter how fast I moved, which, admittedly, wasn't that fast, and how intent I was on the emanations from the box and the thief, I still couldn't catch him. If I'd thought he'd do anything but rip my throat out, I'd have asked Otangu to go get him and kill him this time, but my favor was used up, there would be no second.

So I kept at it, continued moving, and after half an hour I realized something. We were moving away from the crowded city center and into the sprawling outskirts. He must have picked up a vehicle from somewhere as his speed increased dramatically, and with the streets almost empty he got up a good pace and left me for dust.

If this was how he wanted to play it, then I was in. Being sensible this time, I stopped at a twenty-four-hour mini-mart and stocked up on anything I could think of I might need if we returned to the desert. No way would I be caught unawares again. I bought toilet roll, ten bottles of sunscreen, wet wipes, soap, bottles of water galore, and a serious amount of food.

Oh, and I also stole a truck to put it all in.

After loading everything up, I gripped the steering wheel, a knot in the pit of my stomach as I thought about the desert. Maybe that wasn't where he was going. Maybe he would remain in the city. Maybe he wouldn't. It hadn't worked out for him here, he hadn't lost me, had time to fathom the box's mysteries, so maybe he would return to what he knew, where he knew, where he had lived for so long.

It made sense in a twisted kind of way.

He could have any number of secure places out there, his bloody garage would have made a better place to defend than anywhere he could stay in the city.

Stressed, exhausted, unable to think straight with the fear of the desert upon me, I nonetheless started the truck and drove out into the ever-expanding mess of the city where lost hopes and broken dreams kept the impoverished down in the gutter with little hope of ever leaving. Different city, same crap.

We drove around for hours, him turning this way and that, always a mile or so ahead, never stopping for more than a few minutes. Sometimes we drove sedately through shanty towns, sometimes we hit sixty on large open expanses of perfect asphalt. Mostly we headed north, always north.

Soon the buildings and signs of human endeavor faded into the distance. I took a final glance in the rearview mirror and sighed. Here we go again.

There was no denying it now. He was returning to the open spaces he'd made his home while he waited for some numnuts with his prize to turn up and hand it over.

I was definitely too old for this nonsense, and definitely needed a break from the sand and sun. Next holiday I took would be skiing. It would be safer and I could keep all my clothes on.

We turned off the road leading into the city and soon were back on familiar bumpy terrain. I was jostled this way and that as I followed an invisible lead, certain I was on the right pot-holed track. We turned to the east and it was then I became certain we were heading into the desert proper. Back to where this first began with the old man, where he'd built his home.

A huge yellow orb rose over the arid desert and I put my foot down and drove towards the rising sun, cursing as I did so.

I hated this man now. He was screwing with my plans, and those plans were to get out of Africa as soon as possible and never return. Only plus side, it beat jumping from a plane.

Familiar Territory

We drove, and drove, and kept on driving through the early morning, everything the same, everything familiar, yet in truth it could have been anywhere. Sand, sun, heat, although I had air-con this time and oh boy does it make the world of difference when outside you can fry an egg on the roof of your truck.

I necked water like I was trying to drown myself, I tore through the packs of biscuits, dried fruit, and strange snacks I had no idea what was inside but devoured them anyway. I could have eaten for days, grazing non-stop until my belly was fit to burst, but when I glanced at the pile of wrappers on the passenger seat I decided I had better pace myself or I'd be out of supplies before midday.

I drove as fast as I could but it wasn't speedy enough to catch him, which was no surprise. It was like a repeat of the previous chase but this time we were heading away from civilization rather than towards it. Same rules applied though. He knew the roads, or lack of, better, he knew the terrain, and he was less risk-averse when it came to beating the hell out of his vehicle. I played it safe, knew my time would come, and under no circumstances did I want to break down and be stuck out here again. I couldn't face it, was too battle-weary to even contemplate the engine overheating or breaking an axle.

So I followed his dust trail, kept myself amused by dreaming of home, and failed to keep my hands off the lovely snacks.

Time and time again, I cursed myself for letting him get away. I needed to toughen up. Was I going soft in my old age? Normally I would have killed somebody who'd given me a runaround like this without thought. Maybe I saw a potential me in him? That I could be a nutty old guy like this, hanging out in the desert waiting for something to happen. Or maybe I really was more considerate now. Stupid.

We drove on through morning heat and into midday madness, always heading in the same direction. I knew where we were going.

Back to his home, what was left of it.

What surprises awaited me there?

Something nasty, that was for sure.

Finally

Only a few minutes behind him, I slowed as we approached the old homestead. Didn't want those nasty surprises I'd been thinking about for the last day as we made the epic trip back. What was he up to? What would he do? How did he expect to win?

He was powerful, and I got the sinking feeling I hadn't experienced half of what he was capable of. Or had been. With a broken neck? Surely that would put a dent in his powers? I know it would mine. Come to think of it, I was pretty low on the old magic myself. In fact, I don't know when I'd ever felt so empty aside of everything. The desert had abraded me inside and out leaving little but a raggedy shell of a man. Alive, but only just.

As I eased back on the power and drove cautiously towards my fate, I finally took stock of myself now the adrenaline of the chase had worn off. I was dangerously close to death if I didn't take some time out. My body had been bruised, battered, and maltreated beyond its ability to cope and half of me had simply shut down. Movement was sluggish, my arms and legs felt like dead weights, my head throbbed, and my thoughts were slow and muddied. This was no way to enter a battle for the ultimate prize. I should be brimming with magic and feeling super frisky, not on death's door.

What to do? Go for a sleep, top up the magic, have a nice three-course meal and plenty of coffee? I wish. No, this had to be done and it had to be done now. All it took was for him to find a way through the Wards and that would be that. But I needed my magic, now more than ever, so despite my misgivings, I stopped the truck, left the engine running so the air-con kept me cool, and I tried to settle into the Quiet Place.

Easier said than done, and it took a while, but eventually I got to the place that was nothing yet everything, empty yet full, dangerous yet safe, and I let the energy inside me, wallowed in the cold embrace of the infinite, and became a powerful warrior once more.

When I emerged, mind still empty, body adjusting to the newfound strength, it was to find that afternoon had come and almost gone and dusk was soon approaching. He hadn't come to investigate, was probably intent on his prize, or setting a trap or two for the hero, so all was good on that front. There was no sign of anything untoward in the desert, not that I expected there to be, so I shook my limbs back to life, crunched into first gear, and approached the old house.

The other wizards were long gone, probably hunting for us in the city if they'd made it that far, and there was no sign of the old man either. I parked, then clambered out of the truck, ever vigilant for sneaky attacks. It looked the same. A burned-out shell, ash everywhere, dead grass, broken dreams, a life lost. I peered into the darkness of the underground garage where I'd exited, my ears attuned for the slightest sound. Nothing. Was that good or bad? Dunno, but I went to investigate anyway.

Nothing there but cars and machines, the rows of equipment on the racks, same as before. If he wasn't in here then where was he? I checked everywhere, even went back through the tunnel and stared up at the ladder but it was the same. Empty, quiet, unnerving.

Back outside, I searched around but came up empty.

He was gone.

Fine

If he wasn't here, he had to be somewhere else. It stood to reason. Maybe I was overlooking something obvious and he was hiding right beneath my feet, but unless I wanted to, and I absolutely did not, dig up the whole desert, then I'd never know. He could have secret lairs galore but I didn't think so. My instinct, and I learned a long time ago to trust it implicitly, told me he'd returned because he had nowhere else to go, not out of any hope of it offering salvation.

Turned out I was right.

As I wandered, kicking at charred wood and grumbling about the unfairness of life in general, mine in particular, I found him sitting in the remains of his porch, an incongruous sight with him reclining in a chair that was somehow untouched by the fire. How I hadn't seen him before I will never know.

He sat there, calm, like nothing had happened, like he would offer me a nice drink, maybe supper. He looked rough, but the same too. Poised but filthy, thin, with a waxy film to his face, and his neck, oh boy, I don't know how he'd survived, let alone driven here with it at such a weird angle. His head was over to one side and locked slightly back, his shoulder was hunched to meet his ear, and his back was bent awkwardly too. In his lap he cradled the box.

"Game's up, old-timer," I said softly as I approached, senses on high alert.

"Ha, you really gave it to me, Arthur. In all my years, I've hardly ever received even a scratch. Now look at me."

"Can't say I didn't warn you." I pulled up a charred chair and tested it. It held, so I sat opposite him and leaned back. The temperature was perfect as dusk fell. Ash filled my nostrils; magic crackled between us.

"So you did. But what was I to do? I have waited my whole life for—"

"It's your destiny, blah, blah." I waved away his obsession; heard it too many times already.

"What now?" he asked, a glimmer of hope in his eyes like I might still change my mind and let him have it.

"What now? Now you give me the bloody box and I kill you. What else?"

"I was hoping you'd seen the error of your ways, that maybe you would decide to let me have it. I know, I know, I'm a sorry sight, but give me time and I'll be right as rain again, dear boy. This body may look somewhat frail, but I am a fighter and remain powerful. Your magic is no match for mine, Arthur, you would do well to remember that."

"Maybe that was true, but not now, and I'm not the one sitting with a broken neck. It took the vamps minutes to find you, so you aren't that special. But, I have to admit," I scratched my beard with annoyance, "you did give me the runaround."

"Haha, I did, didn't I? Figured you'd get accosted in the back streets, but guess you're tough. I know the places well, from my younger days, and I know the people. Or, rather, they know me. The mad Brit who does magic. They stay away."

"Yeah, but it was a crap plan. You had to keep running, I was always just behind you. What was the point?"

"I knew you'd stop, and you did. I wasn't counting on the vampires. Nasty bunch, no manners, and so unclean." He shuddered, maybe from the cold, maybe because he hated vamps, maybe because he was shutting down.

I saw it, and he knew it too, but still he refused to acknowledge it.

"You look tired, old man. Wait here." I rummaged through the detritus and found what I'd spied earlier. I returned with a thick blanket, only a little burned at the edges, and placed it around his shoulders best I could what with the dodgy neck. I tucked it over his knees then resumed my seat.

"Ah, thank you. My wife made this, it's all I have left of her. Such a good boy, Arthur, I'm sorry it had to come to this. What a life, so much adventure, then so much waiting. Do you know, I only have one regret in this life?"

"Tell me."

"I wish she was still here. My wife. I miss her more than I could possibly explain."

The old man shivered, then cried silently for his wife. Then he died. He just passed away quietly, no drama, no wild outburst, no final attack.

This was why he wanted to return here. It was home. The home he'd made to pay homage to his wife and to wait for something to arrive that finally came. But when it did arrive it gave him no peace or happiness. In the end, he was just an old man in the desert who wished his wife was still with him.

The box fell to the ash-covered sand.

I retrieved it then dug the last grave I would ever dig in the desert.

When he was buried, I stood over his grave and nodded. I knew the shovel would come in handy.

I never did know his name.

Say What?

I milled about for a while, not knowing what to do with myself. To be truthful, I didn't fancy the drive back to the city just yet. Too much had happened, I was too damn tired, and maybe even a little sad too, to even contemplate the long journey. Instead, I gathered as much wood as I could be arsed to carry, then lit a huge bonfire right beside the old man's grave.

Throughout the night, I toasted him, ate my snacks, and stared into the flames for the longest time. At some point, I was nudged awake by something wet at my hand. I opened an eye to find it was my old friend the wolf. How he'd found me over all this distance was a mystery. Guess he was a roamer like me.

"Wanted to get warm, did you?" I asked, reaching out carefully and rubbing behind an ever-alert ear.

He licked my hand.

I rummaged around in the pile of wrappers and found some beef jerky. I settled down on the blanket and he sat next to me, eyes intent on the food. We shared it between us then I curled up on the ground and he eased himself beside me.

Man and beast spooned in the desert to keep each other company through the long night. The fire warmed us both and maybe he was as exhausted as me, I don't know, but we slept until the dawn, him twitching his legs as he dreamed. Maybe I did likewise.

Come morning, we drank water, finished off the jerky, even had a pee together, which was weird, then he wandered off into the desert. He never looked back.

He was right. Never look back, always look ahead.

I gathered up my gear, grabbed some more gasoline from his well-stocked garage, stowed it in the truck, and began the long drive back to Dire Dawa. No, I didn't think about flying again, there would be enough of that later, and besides, I doubted they'd let me on the plane anyway.

Plane Sailing

Close to Dire Dawa, I braked hard and pulled off the road in a shower of dust. I got out of the truck and waited for the mess I'd made to settle. I turned my back on the city and stared into the desert.

"You tried your best, and I think maybe you won this time. I sure feel beat."

The desert had a hold on me, and this was a danger. It gets under your skin and calls like a siren, teasing, promising that if you stay things can be simpler, less complicated, that life out here is all about survival, none of the nonsense like back home. It was tempting, even after everything, but I had a life, family, friends—okay, Vicky—and a lovely kitchen.

Time to go.

I got back in the truck and drove into the city.

Although, I was tempted to go visit Sameena I had to get out of here, and fast. I still didn't know what to do about the box, I was preoccupied with the old guy and what a waste his life had been in the end, and I think maybe I was delaying the shitstorm that would undoubtedly follow when I got back to the UK with such an artifact. It had to be disposed of and quick, before every magical misfit in the country was after me, but I would have plenty of time to come up with something once I was on my way home.

It was with a heavy heart for not saying goodbye to old friends and having a final wander around the city that I arrived at the airport. Darkness was complete now, which seemed apt. The airport was incongruous, gleaming steel and glass after the vastness of the desert.

I stood in line then bought a ticket home, more like a series of tickets, trying not to look too pathetic or keen, but judging by the odd looks I got I failed miserably. Several hours later, after dozing in an uncomfortable chair and ensuring my backpack, complete with priceless artifact, remained clutched tight in my aching hands, I was being shown my seat on a modern airplane, bag still held tight.

We went through the usual crap about us all probably going to die very soon, then seatbelts were buckled, engines roared, and we were heading up into the air even though it's impossible.

I took everything the stewardess could throw at me. Food, drink, those warm lemon-scented cloths to wash your hands with, and I drank so much coffee she ended up leaving the trolley in the aisle beside me for when I wanted another cup.

Several tedious flights merged as I headed home in a daze, and I got increasingly jittery the nearer we got. Was this it? Had I made it? I'd fulfilled Zewedu's last request, the sly old dog, recovered what I'd been sent to recover, and put old ghosts to rest. This part of my life was truly over now. No more would my master haunt my dreams and waking hours, no longer would memories of this particular past leave a sour taste in my mouth. It was done, I was finished, and I'd emerged if not victorious then at least alive.

We arrived in the UK eventually, after what felt like several lifetimes but was merely a few flights with all the accompanying crap. I was queasy from all the foul food and drink, my throat was dry from the weird atmosphere, but at least we hadn't crashed and nobody had blasted out the windows. I hadn't had to jump out either.

After landing, the seatbelt sign clicked off and everyone jumped up to retrieve their bags. I remained in my window seat, left them to it. It's always easier to be last so you don't have to stand awkwardly in the aisle and get whacked by other people's bags.

When there were just a couple of passengers left, waiting same as me, I scooted across to the aisle and made to stand. A small group of Africans came down the aisle and so I moved back in to let them get past. As they shuffled by, I looked up. They were tall, dark even by African standards, and had a strange smell about them. They wore outfits that were ridiculous but not in a funny way. Flip flops, raggedy shorts, t-shirts that didn't fit their frames well.

Then they were gone and I jumped out and headed for the exit.

It was only once I'd disembarked and entered the airport that it suddenly hit me what I'd seen, or rather, who I'd seen.

Tall, slender, well-muscled, smelled musty, almost like death. Looked like they weren't used to wearing clothes.

Oh, fuck.

Vampires!

Trouble in Paradise

As people milled about, waiting in line to go through customs, show passports and explain why they wanted to come into the country, and they better have a good reason, I checked out the passengers, frantic. For some reason, and it wouldn't be a good one, Otangu and several cronies had decided to come visit the UK. It hadn't clicked on the plane, they were past too quickly and the crappy hats hid their faces, but I'd know him anywhere.

I checked everywhere, edged through the crowds trying to find the vamps before they did something terrible, but there was no sign. How the hell can seven-feet-tall vamps hide? Easy. There were several hundred people all packed tight, waiting to get through customs and go pick up their bags.

Aha, bet they didn't have passports, so what would they do? Although, how had they got this far without them? Vampire speed? Bit of glamoring? Something even sneakier?

Panicked, I shoved and barged, shouted and shunted, keen to get to the front before all hell broke loose. These were people from a different time and a very different place and they didn't stand with convention, answered to nobody, had no idea how the modern world worked. They were like babes in that respect, albeit ones with very large teeth.

I shoved two men aside to find myself in that no-man's-land where everyone stands behind a line, waiting for passport control to wave you forward to a counter to stare at you suspiciously and make you feel like you'd done something wrong.

Up at the counter was Otangu and the man and woman he'd brought along. The customs official was red-faced and shouting at them to hand over their passports or they'd be detained. Otangu looked at him blankly then whispered something to the woman. She smiled, her fangs down and gleaming, and as I shouted, "No," she attacked.

It was over the moment it began. The customs guy dropped behind the counter as blood spurted over the woman next to him dealing with an old lady, and the vampire silenced her with a quick tearing out of the throat.

Otangu nodded to the woman and she smiled a sick smile in return; her lips and chin dripped blood.

Pandemonium set in instantly. Everyone went wild, screaming and running back the way we'd just come, so luckily, or unluckily, I was at the rear of it all and didn't get caught in the stampede.

Otangu and his cohorts breezed past the dead and into it the bowels of the airport where countless weary travelers would be milling around the carousels, waiting impatiently for their bag to come out last.

I chased after them, part of me still not believing they were really here, the other part wondering why they'd not waited for me, as I was obviously the reason they'd come.

I sped up as they disappeared around a corner, but the problem with vampires is that they're fast when they want to be, and dangerous at all times. There was no sign of them when I came to a halt in the vast baggage collection area where hundreds of people were entering from all directions to join others keen to escape the airport and move on with their lives.

Then I found them. It wasn't difficult.

Halfway down the room came screams of what could be terror, or could be delight. I followed the sound as I slung the backpack over my shoulders and pulled the straps tight.

"You ready for some action?" I asked Wand as I pulled him from my pocket.

"Is my shaft smoother than your—"

"Just say yes," I sighed.

"Yes." Wand melded into my palm like a sixth finger, familiar and comfortable, where he belonged. Sigils flared, my will joined him in a joyous, if brief, communion, and he burst into crimson life, ready to do battle.

"And don't worry about blasting brains or eyes, you have my permission to destroy these bloodsuckers in any way you see fit."

"Now you're talking. Glad you aren't turning into a lightweight in your old age."

"Who you calling old?" I wheezed as I closed in on the screams.

Nobody was running away though, the news of the deaths hadn't reached this far yet, so what was happening?

I pushed through the crowds gawping at the carousel to find the woman balancing on the conveyor belt, screaming with delight as she slowly went around. She kicked bags out of her way or bent to fling them right across the room, then backtracked when she reached the low bit where bags disappear for several annoying minutes before reappearing.

Otangu and his cohort laughed and clapped at her antics, oblivious to the onlookers.

Before I reached them, a man put his hand on Otangu's shoulder and shouted something.

Otangu's head snapped around, teeth bared. The man tried to backtrack as Otangu laughed but he didn't stand a chance. A moment later his throat was gone and the news that the African vamps were in town spread faster than Vicky could disseminate juicy gossip with a fully-charged phone battery.

In seconds the baggage area was empty of citizens, but I knew that within a minute or less armed police and guards would be swarming the area, keen to shoot anything that looked dodgy.

Without further ado, I raised Wand, focused my will, and let rip with some rather stunning magical mayhem even if I say so myself.

As vermilion magic crackled and wrapped ethereal tendrils around Otangu and the guy next to him, I smiled smugly, thinking this would be over before it even began, but the magic hissed then fizzled to nothing as they darted away just before it made contact.

"What the...?"

"Ah, my friend, you are here," said Otangu with a wide grin. "You forget, we are ancient, and are pure magic, not like your tricks. You will have to do better than that. Our reflexes beat your ridiculous human speed."

The woman hopped down, the three stood side by side, and I answered, "Sure thing," before the battle really began.

Super Annoyed

I blasted again, but Otangu's taunts were true. They were bloody fast, faster than I'd ever seen a vampire move before. No sooner had Wand sent the good stuff right at them than they were well away before it even came close. They could read my body, anticipate my moves, and even if they couldn't, they could still evade the strikes with ease.

Didn't stop me trying, and trying, and trying again.

Already burning out, I took a moment to regroup, and they did likewise. They gathered together beside a pile of luggage, and stood grinning like the twats they were.

"What happened to us being even and you telling me to get lost? What are you doing here?" I asked, already knowing the answer.

"We heard stories," said Otangu.

"After we asked the questions," said the man by his side with an entirely smackable smug grin on his face.

"Oh, and what questions were those?"

"What it was you wanted from the old man. We got several very interesting answers once we gave a little encouragement."

"Yeah, I bet." More death, more bodies, this bloody artifact was nothing but trouble.

"What business is it of yours?"

"We were curious. You were very concerned about its whereabouts, and you called in your favor. I was intrigued. Normally, human worries matter little to us, but in this case..."

"Whatever you think you know, trust me, it isn't like that. Go home, there's nothing for you here."

"That is where you are wrong, my friend, there is something special for us here. We have let you weak creatures have too much freedom for too long. Our time has come and you will help us realize our ultimate goal. We shall take the power, control you all as you should be, so I will have that artifact."

"You don't get it, do you, you fucking idiot. It's too dangerous, too volatile, for you to ever control. You know nothing about magic, wouldn't have a clue how to use it, and even if you could, it would never work how you want it to."

"I'll take my chances. Now, will you give it to me, or are you going to make me angry?"

"What about our deal? We were quits, now this?"

"Quite. We are, as you say, quits. I owe you nothing, so here I am." Otangu held out a hand. I let Wand rip with a quick attack out of desperation but he moved before I'd hardly even thought about blasting him.

"You try my patience, wizard. So be it, you shall die and it will be mine anyway."

"I don't kill so easily, not these days. I'm being careful, watching what I eat, all the good stuff. So, why don't you just bugger off before I do something you'll regret and I'll enjoy?"

"Haha, always the comedian. Just not a very funny one."

It was my turn to anticipate movement, and as they spread out to attack from three sides I did the only sensible thing a wizard could do under such circumstances, I ran.

I leaped luggage and bounced along beside the conveyor belt then dove onto it just before it disappeared through the rubber curtain. Even though I was in mortal peril, I couldn't help but smile. I'd always wondered what happened on the other side, and now I would find out.

"Oh boy," I gasped as I jumped up and put my arms out for balance.

The place was huge, with numerous carousels all spinning around. At the side was a road in the huge underground hangar where small trucks queued to be unloaded. Men chatted idly, others flung bags onto the carousel at superhuman speeds, seemingly in the throes of a game to see who could make the most noise and break the most vacation souvenirs.

A guy taking a sneaky, and no doubt forbidden, drag on a cigarette across the road shouted at me then came storming over.

"You can't be here," he said, "it's not allowed."

"Neither is that," I replied, pointing at his cigarette.

Call it stress, call it withdrawal after weeks of no smoking, or just plain adrenaline getting the better of me, but before I knew what I was doing, Wand was waving about at the guy and his crooked rollie was sailing through the air towards me. I snatched it with my left hand, took a deep drag, felt the nicotine hit relax my muscles, savored the foul taste and the harsh hit at the back of my throat, then was overcome with dizziness after going without my one and only vice, other than killing people, for so long.

Timed to utter imperfection, I heard the rubber part behind me and promptly lost my balance as the nicotine did strange things to my head.

"Get off me, you fucking moron," shouted the guy I'd landed on.

"Sorry, sorry," I gasped, then took another hard drag before stuffing the smoke between his lips and jumping up.

Without looking around, I ran down the road, launched onto the flatbed of a vehicle, then hopped onto another carousel and ducked to get through the curtain.

Something clawed at my calf, and as I emerged into strong light I glanced down to find I was bleeding copiously.

Taking my chance, I blasted through the curtain just as it began to open, then turned and sent concentrated volleys of a Hat special at the turned backs of the vampires.

For once, I was lucky. Otangu sidestepped, but the other guy was a moment too slow and a fat chunk of sheer emptiness hit him smack bang in the chest, sank though, and left a gaping hole. He dropped down, I fired another shot at his head so he couldn't regenerate, and then launched off the carousel and blasted at the crouched woman as she glided through the curtain.

Things Get Dicey

She danced away just in time and landed, cat-like, on a pile of designer luggage. She licked her lips as she advanced, keen for delicious Hat blood.

Otangu shouted something I didn't understand and she nodded. Then she was across the room, giving me a wide berth to join him.

"You dare kill one of us? One of mine!?" spat Otangu, strangely incensed I'd defended myself.

"What, I should have let him suck on me? Are you fucking nuts?"

"We kill you, you do not kill us." Otangu was ultra-angry, like he'd never expected such a thing to happen.

"You're playing with the big boys, nutcase. I told you I was a handful many years ago, that I wasn't to be screwed around, and we had a deal."

"Deal is done, now we fight."

Those weren't the words I wanted to hear. "Why don't we all go home and forget about all this?" was what I wanted to hear.

"I think you're going to have some real trouble on that front," I said, knowing I sounded smug, and not caring.

A veritable platoon of armed men and women came storming into the room through every available door. There were airport security, police with high-vis jackets, and a number of unarmed personnel too. Plus a news reporter judging by how terrified he looked and the phone glued to his ear.

"You need to be taught some manners, all of you do," shouted Otangu, livid. "We will not be interfered with."

And then shit got real. Real nasty.

Airport Carnage

Otangu and his mistress tore around the room like dervishes. Gunfire ricocheted off the walls and the floor, sending shards of tile in every direction. People screamed, others ran, some remained cool under the terrible pressure and tried to find something to aim at. But the vampires were in full-on murder mode and sped from one poor person to the next. I saw the reporter fall under a double onslaught and the woman cackle as she bit deep at his exposed wrist.

A policewoman took the opportunity to fire but the vampire dodged and was on her in an instant, tearing her, literally, limb from limb with sickening snaps that made everyone pause for a moment to stare in utter horror.

It was the opportunity they needed, and the vamps redoubled their efforts. They ripped off heads, yanked off arms, caved in skulls, and eviscerated with a single punch and pull anyone they could find.

It was all so fast, so wild, that you never actually saw it happen, just the aftermath. I didn't have a hope of stopping them, couldn't get a fix on them even though I tried repeatedly, just had to look from body to fallen body and try not to puke.

Then it was done. Almost. Several people wailed or screamed the place down as they stared, aghast, at their limbs next to them in a pool of blood. The vampires weren't quite finished though, and did the rounds once more, just as fast, until the room was deadly silent.

"Now, where were we?" asked Otangu, fondling his assistant in mass murder. Both were soaked though. T-shirts stuck to their firm bodies, their legs were crimson, heads slick with brains and gore. They licked each other like thirsty dogs after a day in the desert. The wildness was upon them, the hold of the vampire complete, and I knew there would be no stopping them now, not alone, not feeling the way I did, not even with full strength.

Running wasn't an option, I'd probably skid on the slick floor and be done for. They had the lust and wanted what was mine.

Aha

Glancing around, I formulated a plan in a split-second, unsure it was the right thing to do.

I grabbed the nearest fallen phone, of which there were many, and hastily dialed a number I never thought I'd use.

"It's The Hat, at the airport. You'll know which one. Bring everyone, and be ready to kill vampires. Ancient, scary, tall vampires." I hung up, hoping I'd made the right decision. There was no going back now, I'd put into action something that would only end one way. It might have been the biggest mistake of my life, it might have been the wisest choice, right now it was the only option I could think of and would have to do.

"You think calling your friends will save you? Haha, you have no idea. You saw what we did, what we can do. Nothing stops us." Otangu stretched out his back then studied me like an insect under a microscope.

"I didn't call my friends. I called my enemies."

The air fizzed and magic cracked reality as a man wearing head-to-toe body armor emerged from the middle of nowhere into the room, a large weapon held out before him. He spoke into the walkie talkie at his lapel then stepped forward. His left hand trailed through the portal. As he moved into the room cautiously, so another man came after him, holding on to the first's sleeve. Then another emerged in the same fashion, then five more, each releasing their predecessor once they were safely through. The next to emerge was Kim, de-facto head of Cerberus, her Hounds before her. She towed a long series of other Hounds behind her, maybe twenty or more in all, each gripping tight to the one in front so the portal remained open and they kept the connection that ensured their safety.

The Hounds spread around the room, weapons trained on both the vampires and me. Kim remained where she was, close to the portal. A metal cylinder was passed to her from the lead Hound which she tucked away into a pocket of her armored vest. The vampires stood their ground, watching, and unnervingly still.

"Arthur," she said with a nod.

"I bloody knew you had another Teleron. You lot are such bullshitters."

"We believed it lost, but it was found. That is no concern of yours. What is the meaning of this? Who are these people? Why have you brought them here?"

"I didn't bloody bring them," I said, incensed. "They followed me. I've been away, in Africa, at—"

"Yes, yes, we know. Dire Dawa. Having an adventure in the desert too, so I hear."

"How do you know?" I snapped.

"We are Cerberus, we know."

"Then you know these freaks are dangerous, and if you don't then take a look around. Care to deal with it before things get out of control?"

"Why should we? This is your mess."

"Because you're here now, and trust me, it will be worth your while."

Kim raised an eyebrow, then frowned as she thought. "Maybe we will. But this is most unconventional. We don't do your bidding, you shouldn't have called."

"I was desperate, and besides, isn't it your job to keep the country safe?"

"That's as may be, but there are police, army, for such matters."

"It isn't their job to fight vampires. And you've been doing plenty of that since you stole so much of Ivan's business. You still dealing drugs now? Become the gangsters I always knew you were?"

Kim scowled. "That's not how it is and you know it. We took what needed to be made right, we are slowly gaining control of the underground, and soon peace shall be restored."

"Yeah, right, good luck with that. You don't know what the fuck you're doing. He won't stand for it." He hadn't been, and the war still raged, but that wasn't my concern. Ivan didn't want my assistance anyway.

"Enough. Let's finish this." Kim turned to the amused vampires and said, "Did you kill these people?"

"Who, us?" smirked the woman.

"Yes, you?"

"Maybe a little," she said, chuckling.

"That's good enough for me." Kim nodded to the lead Hound. He swept his arm forward.

Guns blazed once more.

The Pros are Here

Hounds aren't like the police or airport security, they're more akin to a highly-trained army. They are also utterly indoctrinated into the Cerberus philosophy and feel they are doing almost divine work. In other words, the scariest combination ever. Fanatics with heavy-caliber weaponry.

Hounds are fearless, committed, unafraid of death, or able to hide it well, and better trained than most soldiers. There is certainly more money invested in their training. They have state-of-the-art gear, a solid hierarchy so everyone knows where they stand, and they love shooting the shit out of stuff.

All of this I thought as I stood back and smiled as volley after volley of bullets were directed at the vampires. The initial fire pattern was locked-in and accurate, and the Hounds knew exactly what angle to fire at to maximize damage when the vamps moved but not shoot each other across the room.

Otangu and his cohort were riddled with bullets in an instant, but then things began to break down.

Their wounds were numerous, but they healed almost instantly. Hounds held their fire after the volley and we all watched as the bullets popped out of the vamps' skin and the holes closed up.

"You forget, we are old, and strong. Our companion was young, a mere babe, but we cannot be killed."

"We'll see about that," whispered Kim who had come to stand beside me.

"Yeah, you show 'em," I said, grinning at her.

"Take them," ordered Kim. Her short blond bob haircut swayed, reminding me of those characters you stick onto the dashboard that wobble from side to side. She smelled lovely though, like strawberries, and I couldn't help remember the time I'd seen her naked right before she stole everything Ivan had worked so hard to achieve.

Damn, I needed to get home to Penelope, and fast.

Should I have called Cerberus? It had seemed like a good idea at the time, now it just felt like an idea, not necessarily a good one. Too late now.

The vampires spread apart then were on the move, attacking with all the ferocity they could muster. Several Hounds went down under the onslaught but it was no massacre like earlier. The robust protective clothing they wore meant limbs couldn't be ripped off, teeth or claw couldn't penetrate, and heads couldn't be bashed because of the helmets. Even eyes were protected behind reinforced visors a sledgehammer wouldn't make a dent in.

The vampires howled in frustration as they tore at fabric and battered plastic, sometimes breaking through, more often not, and so they moved on to the next as the Hounds bunched together in small groups and slowly the tide began to turn.

Short burst of gunfire kept the vampires busy regenerating, and all the while the teams closed in, making the wounds deeper, bigger, and more deadly.

Otangu roared his outrage and his lady friend cowered behind him as the teams converged to the front and sides. Stupid mistake. They got cocky and the two proud Africans took their chance. They darted back and then moved in opposite directions at the wall as Hounds opened fire and sprayed wildly, hoping to catch them. Bits of brick and shards of glass littered the floor as the building was demolished, and the teams became two as each hunted a vampire.

Soon the vamps had come full circle, stopping behind me and Kim. The Hounds ceased fire as rapid orders were given and they moved out to resume the attack. Otangu lunged for me as the woman went for Kim but no way was I going out like that after everything that had happened. Wand shone steady and strong as my will exploded in anger into his shaft. He spat gobbet after gobbet of empty death at Otangu who darted this way and that to avoid the barrage.

He was almost upon me before I got a hit. Unfortunately it was only his leg, but he stumbled as flesh and bone was devoured, and then I lucked out as he lost his footing when he kicked into a battered suitcase. He came flying towards me, hands outstretched, face taut with anger. His eyes burned almost crimson with hate and humiliation, so I smiled as I sidestepped and he sprawled onto the tiles.

"We were quits," I whispered as I slammed Wand down with all the fading strength I could muster. Wood tore through Otangu's backbone and kept going until Wand cracked tile beneath the defeated vampire.

Hounds finished him off, fired into his head until there was nothing but splintered bone and mushy brain.

Kim howled her anger as the female vampire clawed at her face. A Hound ripped her away but she readied to attack again.

"Over here," I shouted, and she turned. Her face dropped when she saw what remained of her lover.

Hounds wasted no time and her body and head were riddled with hundreds of bullets. She dropped, the wounds steaming as she fought to recover. She rolled over and clawed her way to Otangu even as Hounds fired and her life force faded.

With an outstretched hand she gripped Otangu's fingers, then her body shook as she was shot yet again before her head exploded as if hit with a sledgehammer.

She twitched several times then was still.

Kim turned to me. "Now, why don't you tell me what this is all about?"

Decision Time

"Oh, I just wanted to catch up, see how you're doing in your new role as Queen Bitch."

"Fine, if that's how it is." Kim turned and barked an order to the Hounds. They were going.

Should I? Shouldn't I? Was this the worst mistake I would ever make? No, my hastily formed plan was the right course of action, even though this would pain me no end and haunt me until the end of my days.

"I found something, in Africa. My old master, his decapitated head kept making me and Penelope jump in the kitchen so I went to Africa to tell him to cut it out and find out what he wanted."

"I am in no mood for your games," said Kim as she turned back to me. She toyed with the Teleron in her hands.

"Where'd you find it? Bet you wish you had another one, eh?" I smiled sweetly, always a winner with the ladies.

"It took a while, and several lives, and yes, if you would return what was ours it would be appreciated."

"You know what they say. Finders keepers, losers take their clothes off and do a little dance." Damn, I really did need to get home, and get Penelope all kinds of naked.

"Idiot." Kim looked at the Teleron then began to adjust it.

"Wait. Um, can we have some privacy? I'll be good, promise."

"If you think I'm going to be alone in the same room as you after our history, then you are a bigger fool than you look."

"I give you my word I won't try to hurt you or do anything mean. I'll be a good boy, promise."

Kim scowled at me then went to talk to her top Hound. She handed over the Teleron then returned to me.

"They have orders to leave then return in five minutes. If I am harmed, they will hunt you and yours until you are all dead. All of you. I mean it."

"Hey, no need to get all moody. I gave my word. A wizard's word is final, I would never go back on it."

"Then the Hounds won't need to destroy your world."

Kim nodded at her men and they all held hands like good Hounds, the lead guy activated the Teleron, then they filed through the magical portal.

"Now, what is this about?"

"No dance first?" Yep, definitely losing it. I was turning into a demented old pervert, if I wasn't already.

Kim slapped me. Hard. I deserved it.

With a sigh, I released my backpack and placed it carefully on the ground. I undid the straps, reached inside, and pulled out the box.

No Remorse

Kim closed the lid gently. She looked at me, eyes wide and full of a million questions.

"Don't ask," I said. "Don't ever ask."

She nodded. "Is it what I think it is?" She was full of doubt yet knew what she held was the true first artifact. The ultimate, nameless prize.

"Yes, so be bloody careful. Look after it, and I mean, really look after it."

"I will. We will. Cerberus thanks you."

"Spare me the bullshit, I'm not in the mood." I rubbed at my face, it felt like sandpaper. The desert had scoured me until I was raw, both inside and out, and I just wanted to go home. I really, really wanted to go home.

"Why us? After all that's happened, why give this to us?" Kim clutched the box tight, and held my gaze with genuine interest.

"Because you're all a bunch of absolute nutters. But I realized something after I carried the artifact across the desert, through the sky, and witnessed the death it caused, the madness it created. I realized that if anyone deserves it, then it's you lot. You know the power this contains, you know what it can do, and you know better than anyone that it can never, ever, be used. So, yeah, Cerberus likes taking artifacts from us adepts, spoiling our fun, so here's one I don't want, that I believe nobody should ever have. Keep it. Now it's your responsibility."

Kim eyed the box nervously. "It will never be taken from us."

"Good. You all got what you wanted finally, something to truly protect. Now you can all feel real smug that you are the caretakers of probably the only artifact you truly deserve. Good luck, you're gonna need it."

I nodded to Kim who returned the gesture.

The air crackled, a Hound walked through the portal, clutching the Teleron tight. They linked arms then left.

Good bloody riddance.

Home at Last

"And I swear I am never, ever, and you have my permission to shoot me if I even suggest it, going back to Africa." The two most important women in my life stared at me, wide-eyed, as I leaned back in the chair and sighed deeply.

I'd been fed, filled with coffee, and got plenty of hugs, but they wouldn't let me sleep until I told them what I'd been up to. There were tears from all concerned, especially me, and I think I might have looked rather a state judging by the fact I only got told off a little and was even allowed two smokes before I regaled my wife and daughter with my tale of woe.

"That's it?" asked George, aghast.

"Nothing more?" asked Penelope, frowning as though disappointed.

"What do you mean? Did you hear what I just told you? How I nearly died, like loads of times? How I jumped out of a plane? How I was attacked by vampires at the airport? That bits of plane fell on me, I wandered the desert for days, got locked in a magical box? C'mon, it was epic. What more do you want?"

"Dad, we heard, and it sounds awful, but you're missing the most juicy bit."

"Huh?" I scratched at my beard to hide my spreading smile. Damn, when would I be allowed to take a shower?

"What was in the box!?" they shouted simultaneously.

"The box?" I asked innocently.

"Yeah, what was the artifact?" asked George, leaning forward, her eyes gleaming.

"Tell us!" shouted Penelope, before she jabbed me in my sore ribs, not that any part of me wasn't sore.

"Ah, well now, wouldn't you like to know?" I grinned, maybe somewhat smugly, then headed off for a shower while two beautiful women shouted after me and threatened all kinds of nasty things, like messing up my cutlery drawer or rearranging my alphabetized cookbook display.

It was good to be home.

The End

Book 12, and it's the big finale, is Sharp Edges.

Get author updates and new release notifications first via the Newsletter at www.alkline.co.uk

Read the Dark Magic Enforcer series for more magical mayhem.